THE COLLECTIVE UPRISING

AWAKENING

Let's connect !

Kayt B

KAYT BRYANS

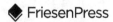 FriesenPress

One Printers Way
Altona, MB R0G 0B0
Canada

www.friesenpress.com

Thank you to Henry David Thoreau - American Author 1817-1862
for providing me with the quote that has consistently reminded me
that the choice of our words and how often we speak them is directly
related to our outlook on life.

Thank you to Dr. Lesley Hannell and Dr. Fred Gallo for the tapping
sequence taught to Maya through Michael.

ISBN
978-1-03-914606-8 (Hardcover)
978-1-03-914605-1 (Paperback)
978-1-03-914607-5 (eBook)

1. YOUNG ADULT FICTION, VISIONARY & METAPHYSICAL

Distributed to the trade by The Ingram Book Company

FOREWORD

THE FOLLOWING STORY is fictional, but many of the strategies discussed within are helpful tools to shift one's perception and experience in life. I have personally used many transformative practices to evolve into my current self. If something within these pages resonates with you, I strongly urge you to do further research to expand your mind and your energy. Seek out the masters and gurus who can assist you with your intellectual and spiritual evolution. You can also swing by my website to see if anything intrigues you there—kaytbryans.org.

With love, light, love and graceful power. ❄♡🙏

WITH
APPRECIATION

"I AM ALL that I have read." Teddy Roosevelt

My knowledge of healing modalities has grown immensely over the past 25 years. It is hard for me to pinpoint many teachings to one specific source. I am grateful for all that I have read and experienced. Reading, journalling, and meditating have been immensely healing for me. I am truly grateful to all of my teachers, masters, and healers. I am specifically grateful to Dean Noblett and Rebecca Couch of Heartlight for guiding me through Reiki mastery so many moons ago; the spiritual teachings of Arrole Lawrence, Aboriginal Healer; the systematic coaching of Alanna Kaivalya from The Kaivalya Yoga Method, and most recently for helping me rekindle my spark and connection; the Ascension coaching of Tara Antler and King Gabriel. I am grateful to Source Energy for the inspiration for this book and the encouragement to continue coming back to the idea that it would become a reality. I am grateful to all of the beings who regularly share their light with the world and who allow me in turn to radiate my light. I am grateful to Dr. Lesley Hannell, of Lesley Hannell

Psychological Counselling for introducing me to a different form of EFT (Emotional Freedom Technique) tapping that I had not seen before. She references this knowledge as likely learned from Dr. Fred P. Gallo. His style of tapping is contained within direct quotes by Michael throughout the chapter titled, "Blocks." I thank every practitioner and supportive practice that has ever contributed to my health and ascension. These include but are not limited to: meditation, chakra cleanses, and breathwork; Reiki, Quantum-Touch and Qigong; yoga, Essential Somatics, and Tai Chi; soul paintings, crystalline energy healing, Sangoma ancestral and traditional healing; Aboriginal healing, iridology, hypnotic past life regression; Raindrop Therapy, and BodyTalk. Thank you to my amazing team at Friesen Press for guiding me in moving my book from a passion to fruition. Last but not least I thank my friends and family for their ongoing support and love. I love you. ☸♡🙏

TABLE OF CONTENTS

Michael	1
Internal Clocks	4
Lost	9
Maya	11
Contact	17
Confusion	23
Commitment	31
Grounding	36
Toying with Time	42
Birthday	49
Gravity	52
In Tune	54
The Pruner	57
Protection	64
Travel Agent	69
Blocks	72
The Next Level	79

Incubation   86

Check-in   97

Co-planning   104

Upping the Ante   110

Filling the Vessel   119

Distraction   129

A Night Off   135

Execute   140

The Search Begins   155

Home   158

What's Next?   162

Meeting Place   164

Finding   170

The Return   175

Recruits   177

MICHAEL

A YOUNG TEEN sits meditating. He looks agitated, or scared, rather than calm. His blonde shaggy hair is swept to the right of his forehead. He appears to be about fourteen years of age.

He is muttering to himself. "Mayday, Mayday, Mayday, we are …"

Michael senses the danger and immediately shifts to a new location.

'Stay calm, Michael, focus!' he says to himself. 'They're close. They're coming fast … but you need to stay calm and focused in order to connect.'

Michael's breathing is heavy. The sound of feet stamping can be heard all around him. He moves in and out of worlds within moments. The scenery changes in a split second. His clothes also change to suit his surroundings. First, he is sitting atop some huge cliffs on a Nova Scotian seashore with wind and crashing water. It feels far too loud and boisterous for Michael. Next, he shifts to a calm pasture, which, at first glance, Michael thinks is perfect, but then he realizes he will be far too open. He settles on a marketplace in the Middle Ages. It is perfect. It's a bustling market with merchants yelling and patrons busily moving about their daily tasks. Michael is now dressed in grubby clothing and fits in as a street urchin.

'At least I am in a busy place,' thinks Michael. 'I will be much harder to find here. No one will be bothered with me if I keep quiet.' His shaggy hair now peeks out from under a cap. He sees a merchant's stall across the market that he can easily crawl underneath without being noticed. As he crosses the square, he stuffs his hat in his back pocket and bends down, pretending to tie his shoe. He huddles here, surveying the surroundings. He looks up at the merchant to ensure he is looking away. When the merchant turns, Michael crawls under the tablecloth. It smells like cinnamon and nutmeg. The stall owner must be selling spices or specialty coffee. Michael crosses his legs and gets comfortable.

'I can still hear the footsteps,' he thinks. 'Maybe they are locals. I know better than to risk it, but I have been running for hours and I'm exhausted.' Michael stays seated under the stall and calmly enters a deep connection, meditating with the intent to warn the others. "Mayday, Mayday, Mayday, we are under attack. We must …"

Within seconds, the shoulder of Michael's shirt is yanked from under the stall.

'The Clippers!' Michael screams internally. 'They've found me!' His connection is lost. He knew the Clippers would find him, but he was hoping to evade their grasp until after he had made the Mayday call.

The Clippers are beasts of men. They are large and muscular, dressed in black and brown leather, with weapons slung around their waists and over their shoulders. Michael struggles against them, but it's no use. One Clipper holds Michael up by his shoulder, while the larger, more grotesque man, with a bulbous nose, clobbers him on the head with a large mallet.

Michael vaguely hears them accusing him of stealing as they pull a bag of cardamom out of his pocket. 'Darn, they're good.' Michael thinks.

The crowd looks at Michael disapprovingly; some patrons even throw garbage at him and start cheering as the Clippers tie his hands together and throw him in the back of a wagon. The shorter of the two Clippers hits Michael a few more times until he blacks out, thus ensuring that he cannot shift to a new location.

The wagon pulls out of the market and drives down the narrow roadway. The Clippers bounce in their seats on the rough rock road. The crowd closes in on the space left by the wagon and the townspeople continue on with their day.

Once the Clippers reach the outskirts of town, they pull over and step down from the seat of the wagon. They check their surroundings to ensure that there aren't any locals nearby. When the coast is clear, the Clippers reach in and drag Michael out of the back of the wagon.

To an onlooker, it seemed as if the three people had disappeared into thin air, leaving an empty wagon on the side of the roadway.

INTERNAL CLOCKS

WHEN MICHAEL COMES to, he is sitting in a dark stone room with his mouth gagged and a Clipper holding up his head. The Clipper has just splashed water on his face and he is still holding the glass a few inches from Michael's nose. Michael shakes his head, trying to shake the water out of his eyes. He is disoriented and looks around at the space, confused.

Michael squints his eyes, trying to remember what had happened. 'Right,' he thinks. 'I got caught in the market.' Michael tries to figure out what time-space reality he is currently in, but he can't quite figure it out. His connection feels blocked. 'Strange.' Michael wonders why this is happening. He has never had this sensation before. Even as a child, when his older brother was teaching him how to locate different time-space realities, he might not have been able to reach them, but nothing ever felt blocked.

Michael looks up groggily to see the face of a bitter and hateful man. He is tall and scrawny with a wispy beard. He looks so frail that he could fall over. He leans over his cane, shaking with fury. Even in his weakness, he towers over Michael.

Michael is baffled as this man appears to be moving in circles over his head. Not so much in a spinning motion, but more like a kaleidoscope. To Michael, he looks like a mirage of a thousand little cruel faces. It is utterly disgusting and frightfully scary.

Michael can hear this man and the Clippers talking about the Community's attempt to overthrow him. Michael tries to figure out what is going on, but it is difficult to focus on their words while trying to calm his blurry vision. 'Focus, Michael!' he tells himself again. Then, Michael heard a word that terrified him. 'Pruner? What? What did he say? Did he just say the Pruner?'

Michael becomes more fearful as the room begins to spin and his surroundings are jumbled. 'The Pruner. This is the Pruner! This is the man I have been avoiding ... and now he has me bound and under his control. Don't panic. It can't be that bad. Just DO NOT PANIC!' Michael tries to calm himself.

Michael hears the Pruner talking about his experience with the Community and how he was shunned from the Community for trying to retain his rightful leadership. He was accused of creating too many rules and using those rules to restrict Community members from living freely. His sentencing allowed the Community to use a powerful meditation technique to hold his internal clock from registering for a year.

"As I'm sure you know Michael, not having access to your internal clock means you cannot shift to different time-space realities." The Pruner pauses for effect. "A whole year," he gasps, as if he is putting on a show. "I had to stay in one location!" He hobbles across the room, then turns back, pointing an accusatory finger. "Your precious Community did this. I had not stayed in one location for more than a few days since I had learned the art of meditation and shifting in my early teens," he yells in disgust. "When my internal clock was restored to me, I vowed that no one would ever again be able to control my shifting." He goes on to explain how he has designed an intricate tool that is more powerful than meditation. It has the ability to actually remove a person's internal clock, separating it from a person and locking it away in a separate location.

Michael tries to shout. A Clipper laughs at his attempt and steps closer to remove his gag. "Remove people's internal clocks?" Michael shouts in shock, "But that's immoral! Connection is a basic human right!"

The Pruner grows taller and peers down his nose. He leans forward on his long, crooked cane and snickers. He goes on to explain that once he had the tool, all he needed was employees to carry out his evil plan. He was intending to abduct as many Community members as possible, starting with the ones who were trying to warn the Community. The Clippers were hired to track down these poor souls. They were scouted from all different time-space realities and tribes to work for him on the pretense of keeping their internal clocks intact. Their fear was real, and blackmail was definitely an effective way to keep these people working. He said Michael had popped up on his radar as a supporter of the Community.

"Which leads us here, dear Michael," his voice sounds slimy, and it slithers into Michael's ears as he draws out the words, "Would you like to see my miraculous tool?"

Michael shakes his head and tries to push back, violently attempting to fight off the Clippers. He wriggles and kicks, feeling their grip get tighter. Michael doesn't stop fighting and winds up with another welt on his left temple. While the blow is painful, a punch is not nearly as frightening as tampering with one's internal clock. Michael continues to fight—rage and fear welling up inside him.

The Clippers are big men who laugh at Michael's attempts. They pick Michael up like he's a sack of potatoes and carry him over to a wooden table where they throw him down and hold him in place. The Clippers use leather straps to tie him down at the wrists, ankles, forehead, and waist. Michael tries to squirm out of the straps on the table. The wooden slab does not give, and the straps get tighter with each attempt. The Pruner cackles as the Clippers tie off the ends of the straps.

Panic-stricken, Michael watches the old man pull out an object that looks something like a large needle set inside a suction ring with four ominous metal bracing arms. He slowly steps toward Michael, as if performing a giddy dance. He steps a little closer and giggles like a child. When the Pruner looks to the Clippers, one reaches in a tears Michael's shirt open. The Pruner places the contraption near the centre of Michael's sternum, then he repositions it further up. He pushes it down into Michael's torso, trying to get a seal. Michael pants louder, screams, and shakes beneath its force. Michael can only move mere inches on the table, but it is enough to delay this hideous machine from connecting. It's only a matter of seconds before they attach the suction ring. He cannot get away. 'Panic!' Michael screams to himself. 'This is the time to *panic!*'

The Pruner repositions the machine onto the exact centre of Michael's chest, pushing down hard. The suction ring takes a deeper hold of Michael's skin and the metal bracing arms pinch his shoulders and ribs. The Pruner pushes hard into the handles, compressing Michael's chest cavity. The pressure is immense. It feels as though his ribs are breaking. Michael can see the needle descend into the ring. His eyes are open wide as he watches, fear-stricken. It feels like slow motion. Michael has a very good idea of what is about to happen, but he cannot fathom that it is actually happening. Sweat beads on his upper lip.

Eventually, the needle pierces through the centre of Michael's chest. The noise is so loud, it sounds like a giant hole punch, jabbing into his chest. The pain and the intensity are too much. Michael sinks into blackness for the second time today.

LOST

MICHAEL WAKES UP shivering. It is very dark, and colder than he has ever experienced, yet there is no snow or ice.

'This is a strange place,' Michael thinks. 'Foreign on all accounts. I cannot remember coming here.' Michael glances around. It looks like it must be an abandoned town. The buildings seem deserted and are crumbling. The town feels old and destitute, and yet it appears newer than Michael's natural time-space reality. 'Why did I come here?' Michael stands, wobbling and sore. He stumbles forward. He doesn't feel well, and thinks he's going to be sick. Michael bends over, leaning on a crumbling bench for support. He heaves twice and grabs his stomach, groaning. He shakes his head and tries to stand up to walk it off. He looks around in awe. 'This place,' he thinks. 'It's like nowhere I have ever been. How did I get here?'

"Hello?" Michael yells. "Is anybody here?" He listens into the abyss. "Hello?" he screams at the top of his lungs. Michael's voice echoes down the street. There is no reply.

Michael tries to remember his path to this place. His mind is foggy and he can't seem to grasp what has happened. He finds a spot to sit down to connect. Michael knows that meditating is the fastest way to figure any-thing out.

As he sits, he thinks of his older brother. He's the coolest person Michael knows; he can do everything. He can easily meditate anywhere, while doing anything. He can be walking down the street, humming a tune, and still be connected on a deep level. Michael, on the other hand, has to find a comfortable place to sit down and focus his attention inward. He can still hear his mother's voice: "Michael, you cannot be jealous of Gabe. He is at a different stage of growth. Plus, jealousy is the root of all evil." Michael laughs at the memory of his mom saying the ancient quote that seems to be thrown around a lot in his town.

As Michael settles into his meditation, he is suddenly discomforted by the fact that not only can he not connect to the Collective Community, but he also can't reach his inner self. As he tries harder to focus, he feels a deep pain in his chest and memories flood his periphery. Michael is shocked and hurt, recoiling from the memory. 'Oh, my goodness! My internal clock has been removed!' Michael screams to himself in anguish. He remembers the Pruner's horrific face as he jabbed him with that needle. The old man's laugh, and his vow to find and destroy all of the Community members. His vehement hate was palpable. 'That man is crazy,' Michael thinks. 'I have to do some-thing … But what? I need to contact the Community members … But how?"

MAYA

MAYA IS SITTING in the corner of a hallway in her middle school, eating her lunch—California rolls. She is using chopsticks to mix the wasabi and ginger in the soy sauce. It's one of her favourite lunches that she rarely gets. Her mom must have sent it as a special Friday treat.

'I can almost taste it.' Michael drools as he imagines the feeling of the wasabi burning his eyes and nostrils. Michael wipes his lips. 'Oh man, I am totally drooling. I haven't eaten a real meal in ages ... what literally feels like ages.'

He is observing Maya. She is a typical student from what he can see ... with untypical hair. It's long and wavy, fiery and red. Red as flames. She's reading. She's sporting glasses. Not in a nerdy way—they are sort of cool—or at least they seem to add to her style. She is clearly not popular, but he doesn't think she would be targeted for tormenting. She appears sweet and endearing. She shovels another piece of sushi into her mouth. She looks up every once in a while, shyly smiling while glancing around to see if any classmates are walking by. She looks hardworking and slightly athletic. Friendly. Sociable, but a bit of a loner.

'She's perfect,' Michael thinks. 'What is she reading? Hmm, science … useful … and war crimes ... excellent.' Michael tries yelling at her, "Maya!"

As the bell rings, Maya scrambles to pack up her things quickly and shove one more piece of sushi into her mouth. Maya thinks she hears it … her name being called. She chews frantically, collecting her books and bag and looks around. Funny—there is no one else in this hallway. Everyone has already raced to their afternoon class. She swallows hard and peers around one more time before hurrying off down the hall.

"She heard me. She actually heard me! Whoo hoo!" Michael yells into the abyss of his world of nothing-ness. "Yes!"

As the end of day bell rings, Maya is excited for her walk home. She rushes to her locker to drop off some of her things, passing a few acquaintances and saying hi as she quickly unzips her backpack and unlocks her lock. She leaves one of her books on the top shelf and grabs her water bottle. She is already daydreaming. Her mind appears to be working overtime as her eyes dart from side to side and up and down as she calculates an angle in her mind. She is going to stop by the local junk shop. They have great deals on everything. One bagful of stuff is five dollars. Any time! It's really quite amazing. It's a tinkerer's dream store. 'I bet I can make a whole new roller coaster out of the things that I find today,' she thinks. 'It's going to have a loop the loop and a steep climb with a crazy

swooping curve rushing toward the ground. How cool!'
She pauses to create another calculation in her mind. She
imagines actually being able to make real roller coasters.
What an awesome gig! She pauses as if trying to convince
herself. 'I could become an engineer. A roller coaster engineer! Yeah! How cool would that be! Who needs rocket
scientists when you have roller coaster engineers? Well,
both are good careers, but roller coasters are way cooler!'

Maya has always dreamed of becoming a scientist or
an engineer one day. While she likes to build strange con-
traptions in her spare time, her passion is definitely the
momentum. The creations are grand displays of flair, and
there is always a path of inertia that engages the audience.
Each new piece of construction allows her to fine-tune
her skills and develop a better understanding of how far
she can push the materials.

As Maya walks into the store, she waves at the shop-
keeper. "Hello Mr. Clark," she calls as she weaves her way
around the baskets of collections, heading to her favourite
part of the store first.

"Hi Maya! Welcome back! I have some cool new
tunnels for you today. I'll just finish up with this invoice
and I'll meet you in the back," Mr. Clark responds.

"Sounds good. I'll be in the piping section." Maya
smiles, knowing Mr. Clark likes to contribute to
her creations.

'Piping is her favourite section.' Michael recalls. 'She
goes there first every single time.' Michael has been
keeping an eye on Maya for a couple months now, while
scouting out other prospects. He knows her daily routines

and has been watching intently as this newest roller coaster has developed. While she loves the texture of each piece, she is also drawn to the sounds each tunnel makes. There is a slight vibration to the pipes. Michael is not sure if she even realizes she is doing it, but each time Maya inspects a piece of piping, she holds it up to her ear for a glimmer of a second. It's as if she knows that everything has a frequency. 'Maya's personal frequency is high today. I will try to contact her again … Maya!'

Maya pauses ever so slightly as she listens to a piece of piping. She blinks and frowns. This piece sounds sad, like a low hum. All of a sudden, she hears her name again. She looks around again … feeling uneasy. She is about to say hello when Mr. Clark comes around the corner of the aisle and starts walking toward her.

"You found our new pieces?" he asks.

"Yes, thanks for the heads up. I love this piece," Maya responds.

"Yes, it is a very unique piece. It naturally has these waves in it and the metal is very light. There are two more similar pieces over here." Mr. Clark moves slightly farther down the aisle to grab the other pieces of retired piping. "What do you think you will use them for?"

"I am thinking of creating a new roller coaster today. I need to take a break from the last one. I have some fresh ideas I want to play out. I have been thinking a lot about frogs lately and I think there is a themed ride somewhere in my thoughts." Maya rambles as she digs through the baskets.

Mr. Clark looks a little confused. "Frogs? Okay. Have fun with that!"

Maya takes the other two pieces of piping and turns down the next aisle. She wanders aimlessly for the next few minutes, picking up seemingly random objects and either placing them in her bag or discarding them after a quick inspection. When her bag is full, she walks up to the front counter with her five dollars in hand, ready to pay. "Thank you so much Mr. Clark. I found some great materials today; I can't wait to get started!"

"Have fun Maya!" he said, "Ribbit, ribbit!"

"Ribbit, ribbit?" Maya questions, squinting her eyes in confusion at Mr. Clark.

"Your frog thing … ribbit, ribbit." he says with a sheepish smile.

"Oh right! The frog says ribbit. Too funny!" She giggles, thinking she really needs to grow up as she saunters out of the store. She thinks about the guttural sounds frogs make and she begins to hum. "Hum, aum, om." She thinks it's interesting that the frog sound is similar to what she heard in the pipe.

'In finding the frog sound she has already tapped into the basic sound of the whole universe. She is going to be so strong … if only I can contact her!' thinks Michael.

As Maya walks home, she continues to play with the different sounds that she thinks a frog might make … a croak, a growl, a cluck. She comes back to the hum as she runs in the front door, intent on beelining it to her workshop in the basement, when she is interrupted.

"Maya," her mother calls. "Come here please."

Maya's mom is in the kitchen, cracking an egg. She's pretty, she has clear skin with laugh lines beginning to form and a few wrinkles around her mouth. Her hair is mostly blonde with some red highlights and a few grey hairs starting to come in around her face. She looks tired but upbeat and happy to see her daughter.

"Yeah, Mom?" Maya answers, out of breath and extremely excited to start working on her roller coaster.

"How was your day, love?" her mom asks as she pulls Maya close and kisses her forehead. "What was the best part?"

"Great mom! During recess, I read this cool book about the genetic makeup of toads and frogs, and I stopped by the junk store and picked up some fun stuff to start a new roller coaster … Do I have time? Before dinner? To work on it a bit? Pleeease?"

"Okay, silly. Go have fun. I'll call you for dinner in a bit." Her mom turns back to the counter to batter the fish.

'Oh, the fish … even fish smells good at this moment. I can't wait until I can eat delicious food again!' Michael's gaze follows Maya as she crosses the room.

"Thanks Mom!" she giggles as she hugs her again and runs down the stairs.

CONTACT

MAYA EAGERLY EMPTIES her bag of goodies onto her workbench. She tinkers with each piece, positioning and repositioning them until they start to resemble a miniature roller coaster. At one point, she leans over to turn on her soldering gun and the fan that sits next to it. While she putters, she begins to hum ... each time she hums, the frog croak begins to sound a bit more like om. Michael continues to try to contact Maya during her explorations, but she is focused on her creation and he can't seem to break her train of thought. Before long she is called to dinner and Michael decides he needs a rest.

'I am making progress,' he thinks. 'She is starting to hear. I need to keep the faith that she is unconsciously opening her connection and will soon hear me.'

After dinner, Maya heads over to the park to read. She climbs into her favourite tunnel and takes out her most recent library find titled, *War Crimes*. She is enjoying reading about how leaders maneuver their troops to outwit their opponents. True victory seems to lie in the planning stage and intelligence, as physical combat has too many avenues for errors and foiled offensive tactics. While intently reading, Maya hears her name again, and looks startled as she peers out of the tunnel.

"Maya!" Michael mentally screams. "Maaayaaa!"

'No, really,' Maya thinks. 'I swear I heard it that time.'

"You did!" confirms Michael.

"I did?" Maya responds, looking frantically from side to side.

"Yes, and I have been trying to contact you for a while now."

"Where are you?" asks Maya, continuing to look around.

"Shhh! Just think it. I'm speaking directly to your mind," Michael says.

"Oh, my goodness. I'm going crazy. I'm talking to myself. Mom is going to love this one," Maya chides herself under her breath.

"You're not talking to yourself. My name is Michael. I have a skill of communicating through your mind. Act normal and pretend to read or people will think you *are* crazy. Just think about what you want to say to me."

"Uh, okay. So, you mean to tell me that it was you? All those times that I thought that I heard my name, you were calling me?" Maya replies.

"Think … don't say!" Michael chastises.

"Oh right! Oops! Okay," Maya thinks.

"Excellent! Very exciting! It is so important that I made contact with you. I have not been able to contact anyone for a very long time. This is amazing! It feels so good to talk to someone." Michael sounds as though he is beaming.

"You don't have anyone to talk to where you live?" Maya questions.

"Well, I am barely living at the moment. I was sent … wait … too much information. Maya, I know a lot about you because I've been watching you and I've been trying to communicate with you for many weeks. But you know nothing about me," Michael says.

"Creepy! What are you? A stalker?" Maya scrunches her face at the scary thought.

"No! Not at all … it's complicated. As I said, my name is Michael. I am fourteen years old. My family lives in the modern time-space reality but not as recent as your years … nearly a century before your time."

"Wait. What? Time-space reality? What is that? And you think a hundred years ago is modern?" scoffs Maya.

"First things first. A time-space reality is the moment at which you find yourself at any given moment. You don't always need to stay in your current life timeline. It's possible to shift between years and places based on your thoughts," says Michael.

"Are you crazy? As if!" Maya shakes her head.

"No, really Maya. When you are ready, I will teach you, but for now, please do not even try it — it could be dangerous for you to travel at this time." Michael cautions.

"Dangerous, how so?" Maya probes.

"Well, as I was saying, I am from a time-space reality about a hundred years before you. My family comes from a long line of connected beings. Nowadays, we can all learn to connect, but my family learned to connect early on in their lifetimes. Naturally, we are all shifters, but most people have forgotten. My brother and I were trained to shift from a very young age. We learned that we have the ability to both meditate to connect to our higher self and the higher self of others, but also to shift time-space realities and to communicate with all other beings on the planet or in the galaxy." explains Michael.

"Whoa! How did your parents learn that they had this ability?" asks Maya.

"Hmm, I am not sure ... I mean, I don't remember exactly. My mom had a mentor who initially introduced her to the basic skills, but she is a force to be reckoned with and she expanded her understanding with more meditation and practice. My parents have been teaching me since I was little. I am still training myself. Unfortunately, I was trying to send a warning out to my family and the Collective Community when I was caught by an evil man attempting to shatter our ability to communicate in this way," says Michael.

"Oh no! Are you okay?" questions Maya.

"No, not really. I will survive for a little while longer, but I am living in a destitute place with very little food. I have been living off bugs and rodents and I am not even sure how they got here. I have an urgent message that I need to get out to the masses and I need you to help me," explains Michael.

"Me? But I don't really know how to meditate!" Maya lifts her hands in exasperation.

"I can help you," assures Michael. "Look at the conversation that we are already having … and that is without any experience!"

"Good point!" Maya exclaims. "What's next?"

"Well, it is going to take practice," Michael continues. "You have some basics you need to learn first, and you're not ready to send a mass message. I need to teach you some defense mechanisms so that you don't get caught by the same people who found me."

"Okay. What do I have to do first?" Maya takes a deep breath.

"First, I want you to have a normal evening," Michael says. "Think about this conversation and know I am here to support you. But you also need to know that what you are volunteering for could be very dangerous. Not only for you, but also for your close friends and family. However, by agreeing to help me, you will be an integral part of saving many lives, including, potentially, my own."

"You might not survive?" asks Maya in disbelief.

"I'm not sure, Maya; there isn't a lot of food here. I'm hoping you will be able to find me at some point and that I can survive until that day," explains Michael.

"Okay. That's big!" Maya responds. "What else?"

Michael examines Maya's response and energy to determine how ready she is and how well she is digesting this information. He pauses and scratches his left eyebrow. "Come back here tomorrow with something comfortable to sit on, snacks, a book, and a pair of dark sunglasses. That way, you can pretend to read and no one will notice that your eyes are closed," he tells her.

"Got it!" Maya says as she stands and starts to collect her things.

"Great. And Maya …" Michael adds.

"Yes?" Maya smiles.

"It's wonderful to finally get in contact with you. I'm truly relieved. I don't mean to scare you, but I'm super stoked at the possibility of working with you," Michael shares.

"Truthfully, I'm a bit overwhelmed," Maya admits, "but I guess I should thank you for choosing me."

"It's fate!" Michael exclaims. "I think you have the ability to be very powerful. Let's chat tomorrow. Have a great night!"

"You too Michael, you too!" Maya grins as she walks away from the park.

CONFUSION

MAYA TAKES THE long way home. She knows it is getting late, but she needs more time to think. She debates whether she should tell her mom.

Maya opens the back door and goes into the mudroom. "Hi Mom! I'm home!"

"Hi love! I'm in the kitchen," Mom responds. "There are some washed berries on the table if you want a snack."

Maya drops her books in a cubby and heads into the kitchen. Her mom looks at her and says, "You're awfully late tonight ... anything fun happening at the park?"

"Yeah, sorry Mom. I got caught up reading." Maya sits down at the table and looks at her mom. "Mom, is there any time that hearing voices is not crazy?" she asks.

Distracted by the dishes, her mom says, "Um, I guess so. Why? Are you hearing voices?" she looks over her shoulder and asks in a pandering voice.

Maya giggles and sidesteps the question. "No, I was just wondering. I heard that sometimes people pray and hear the response, or that they hear themselves respond."

"Well darling, I chat to myself all the time and you don't think I'm crazy, do you?" Mom chuckles.

"No Mom; just a little quirky." Maya grins as she sticks out her tongue. She picks up a raspberry and pops it in her mouth.

"Right back at you, love!" Mom winks and reaches for the dish towel.

Maya continues to eat quietly, rolling the raspberries onto the tips of her fingers like when she was a child. She stares at the berries pensively and ponder her conversation with Michael.

"Truthfully, hearing voices gets a bad rap when discussing people's mental health, but there are a couple ways to look at it," Mom offers.

Maya looks up mid-chew.

"For instance, you've probably seen a cartoon or skit where there is a little angel or devil on someone's shoulder," Mom says.

Maya nods. "Oh yeah, I do remember watching a TV show about that when I was little. There was a devil on the girl's shoulder. Truthfully, I'm not sure I really understand the analogy, though."

"Well, the idea is that the good choices in you and the bad choices in you are having an argument. They are each trying to win you over to their side. When you choose to do something bad, you are siding with the metaphorical devil, and when you choose to do something good, you are choosing the side of the angel," Mom explains.

"Oh! That makes sense." Maya nods. "It's never been completely explained, and I didn't quite make the connection."

"Ah," Mom grins. "That's understandable. Any time cartoons are involved, the content can often be glossed over. The cartoon looks so cute, but the theory is that the devil controls hell and he is trying to convince you to do something that you know you shouldn't do. Whereas the angel represents everything good in you, and when you choose to do the right thing, even when no one is watching, you are being sort of angelic."

"Ooh!" Maya laughs. "That's a great way to look at it."

"The other way I hear voices, when I think it is okay, is when I'm journalling or meditating," Mom continues. "When I need an answer to a question and I can't seem to figure it out and I want to get my 'thinking' brain out of the way, I like to journal. First, I write down everything that is in my mind. They can be silly or frustrating thoughts. They can be judgments I hold about myself or situations that have happened that I can't seem to let go of. I write until there is nothing left that I am stuck on or thinking about. Then, I crumple up that piece of paper and throw it away and start a fresh piece of paper. On this page, I write the question I want answered. Usually, by the time I finish writing the question, the answer has popped into my mind and flows through my writing hand. It's quite amazing, really. This technique also works by meditating. I've mentioned it to you before, but perhaps you weren't ready to hear it. You start by finding your inner calm. Take some deep breaths and slow your breathing down. Then, ask yourself the question you are hoping to find an answer for. After you ask, sit quietly, and wait for the answer."

"Oh, that's cool. What if an answer doesn't come?"

"If you are patient and calm, answers almost always come. If they don't, you might not be ready for the answer, or perhaps you haven't been able to get calm enough … so take a break and try again later. There is one other technique I like to use for big issues that I can't seem to figure out the answer to," Mom mentions. "Would you like to hear about it?"

"Yes please," Maya adds "I have a big conundrum that I am working through."

"Do you want to share? Or just try this style of meditation?" Mom asks.

"I just want to try the meditation, please," Maya assures her.

"Okay, this is one of my favourite meditations for diving into my subconscious." Mom starts, then pauses. "Do you know what subconscious means?"

"It's something to do with the brain, right?" Maya says honestly with a grin.

Mom nods. "Yes! When you are aware of something, for instance this room, or your positive thoughts about the taste of ice cream, that is conscious thought. You know you are having them. These thoughts are part of your consciousness and awareness. Does that make sense so far?"

"Yes," Maya nods.

"When you have thoughts that you don't realize you are having, these are called subconscious thoughts. These are thoughts that are beneath the surface or thoughts that you are unaware of." Mom simplifies. "For example, sometimes when you are doing gymnastics you get a feeling you shouldn't try something, for some reason. You're not sure why, but you step away. You won't necessarily ever know what you were thinking because it was subconscious, underneath your knowing, but it might have been intuition that the surroundings were not safe, or self-doubt that you could complete the move. Another way we have subconscious thoughts is through the chatter we hear every day. Our brain is constantly taking in its surroundings. Everything our eyes and ears pick up, like watching or listening to shows and music. Even if we aren't specifically paying attention to what's going on around us, our brains are constantly filtering information, whether we realize it or not. We are taking in everything that we come in contact with every single day. These ideas are sinking into our brain, and each day we have both conscious and subconscious thoughts.

"Sometimes, if we want to access our subconscious thoughts, we have to get out of our own way by quieting our conscious mind. You can think of it as your intelligence and knowledge blocking your access to your deeper thoughts. So, this meditation," Mom explains, "dives deeper. You will sit calmly and breathe first. Then you will ask yourself, 'What do I know about this situation?' I find it helpful to tap my forehead, as if accessing my brain. You can ask the question until the answer comes to you.

Mom pauses to demonstrate, asking herself the question three times, "What do I know about this situation? What do I know about this situation? What do I know about this situation?" while tapping her forehead.

"Once you get the answer, ask the next question, 'What do I feel about this situation?' while tapping or holding your heart. Remember, you can ask the question as many times as you need to until you get an answer, but three times is a good starting point." Again, Mom demonstrates tapping her heart with her whole hand and asking herself the question three times. "What do I feel about this situation? What do I feel about this situation? What do I feel about this situation?

"Thirdly, you will touch your throat or your lips and ask, 'What do I need to communicate about this situation?'" Mom pauses one final time to place her fingertips on her lips and ask herself the question three times. "What do I need to communicate about this situation? What do I need to communicate about this situation? What do I need to communicate about this situation?

"Sometimes, with this last question, you won't actually need to tell anyone what your answer is. Sometimes it is communication just for you. At other times, you will know if you need to tell someone or explain something to someone."

"And you always get an answer?" Maya looks up incredulously.

"I have always gotten an answer, Maya." Mom smiles.

"That's really cool." Maya grins.

"Yes, it is!" agrees Mom. "Do you want to try it together?"

"Hmm," Maya stalls. "Not yet; I might try it later."

"Sounds good. Why don't you go work on your new roller coaster for a bit while I tidy the kitchen, and then we can go for a walk before bed," Mom suggests.

"Sure," Maya responds absently, and walks toward the basement stairs. She hums as she walks downstairs. She looks around the basement distractedly and sits down in front of her roller coasters. Maya sits quietly as if she is staring into a void. Her mind is equally paused and racing at the same time.

'What should I do?' she mulls. 'Safety versus danger? Nothing versus the right thing to do? Familiarity versus the unknown? Placing my family in jeopardy versus saving many families?'

Maya takes a few deep breaths and places her fingertips on her forehead. She asks herself, "What do I know about this situation? What do I know about this situation? What do I know about this situation?" She waits less than a second. *You know this is the right thing to do.* 'Yes, I do know that.' Maya grins.

She places her hand on her heart. "What do I feel about this situation? What do I feel about this situation? What do I feel about this situation?" *I am scared. But I feel like I can make a real difference.* 'I can! This is such a cool exercise!'

Lastly, Maya places her fingertips on her lips. "What do I need to communicate about this situation? What do I need to communicate about this situation? What do I need to communicate about this situation?" *You need to tell Michael YES! You need to be vague with your mom so that she doesn't figure this out or she'll worry.* Maya nods. 'So cool!'

With her mind clear, Maya shakes her head and focuses on her new frog roller coaster. She hums while she works. When her mom calls down to go for a walk, she is just adding the final new pipe into the mix. She steps back, proud of her progress today. Maya turns and dances up the stairs.

On their walk, Maya thanks her mom for the meditation tip. She says she did get an answer and she feels much better about it. She was able to leave it at that and redirect their conversation to her new roller coaster, getting hyped up about the frog symmetry, the loops around the legs and tongue and how the riders will hear the humming croaks as they whisk around the loops.

After their walk, Maya heads up to bed. It's late, but that is fairly common for a Friday night; however, she wants to wake up rested and energized for a busy day of learning.

COMMITMENT

MAYA WAKES UP early and throws off her duvet. She has lots of time, but she wants to get to the park as soon as possible. She switches out of her romper pajamas and pulls on a comfortable pair of yoga pants, a tank top, and a zip-up sweatshirt. She grabs a book, her tablet and some headphones to put in her bag—just in case. She quickly pulls her hair back into a ponytail and starts to braid it as she skips downstairs. She is twisting the last loop of her hair elastic as she walks into the kitchen. Her mom is in the living room, practising yoga. Perfect … minimal distractions. Maya quietly grabs a yogurt, a granola bar, and a banana to put in her backpack.

"Good morning, darling," Mom calls to her. "Where are you off to so early this morning?"

"Good morning! I'm really into this book about frogs. I'm going to go read in the park again." Maya makes a lame excuse, hoping her mom doesn't push.

"Okay. Have fun … and be safe!" Mom chortles.

"I know, I know." Maya walks in to kiss her on her forehead.

"Be back by four at the latest," Mom reminds Maya.

"Will do!" Maya calls as she runs out the door. She tries to bike faster than fast over to the local park. Maya quickly locks her bike and runs to the top of the hill near the park where she had chatted with Michael yesterday. She lays out a blanket haphazardly with her snacks and lies down with her book while she waits.

It took less than a minute for Michael's voice to chime in her head, "Good morning, Maya! You're here earlier than I expected!"

"Good morning, Michael!" Maya eagerly responds while sitting up.

Michael wastes no time and asks, "Did you make a decision?"

"Yes!" Maya exclaims. "I realize that this may be danger-ous, but I know it's the right thing to do and that it may save many people from harm."

"Excellent," Michael returns. "That's a great perspective. First things first, Maya. In the beginning, when learning to meditate, it is best to sit up straight with your legs crossed."

Maya repositions herself and waits for the next instruction.

"That's great, Maya," Michael says calmly. "Now, straighten your spine and think about raising the top of your head up to the sky. Feel your sitz bones pressing into the earth."

"My sitz bones?" Maya questions.

"Yes, the two bones that stick out of your bottom ... they are the bones at the lower part of your pelvis that you feel pushing into the ground," Michael describes. "You might need to pull your thighs or fleshy bits of your bottom out of the way to feel them."

Maya tilts her hips and leans forward a bit, moving the fleshy bits of her muscles out of the way until she can feel her sitz bones.

"This is not very comfortable, Michael," she complains.

"No, it's not at first," Michael agrees, "but you will learn to overlook your physical sensations. Okay, now that you are in position, I want to do a couple of quick exercises with you. Remember, I am moving quickly because time is of an essence, but I don't want you to miss anything. If you have any questions, please do not hesitate to ask."

"Sounds good," Maya agrees.

Michael's tone of voice changes and he quietly begins to guide Maya into a deep state of relaxation. "Start by closing your eyes. Take a deep breath in through your nose and let a big sigh out through your mouth. Again, inhale through your nose, and exhale, letting out a big sigh."

Maya's second sigh is audibly different. She is clearly relaxing deeper.

"One more time," Michael continues. "Inhale through your nose, exhale sigh." Maya's shoulders visibly sink and relax on this third sigh. "Now breathe a bit more normally, in and out through your nose. Inhale, two, three, and exhale, two, three. Inhale, two, three. Exhale, two, three. Start to feel the space around you."

"Huh? Close my eyes and feel the space around me?" Maya questions. "Like, with my hands?"

"No," Michael responds with a quiet chuckle. "Like, with your mind!"

"Oh, okay. How do I do that?" Maya scrunches her eyes closed tighter, then opens them in confusion.

"Close your eyes. We'll practice together. As you sit there, I want you to explore the space by leaning forward … and back … to the left and to the right. Now, sitting tall, imagine a bubble is around you. It's approximately six feet in diameter. Try to feel the emptiness of this sphere." Michael pauses to allow Maya to sense the emptiness.

"Now try the opposite; try to imagine or feel this sphere with a sense of fullness. Picture white light filling your whole body. Now imagine this light pushing through the barrier of your skin and filling your whole bubble. Allow the light to swirl all around you, pushing up against the outside of the bubble—so full it's ready to burst." Michael waits another moment, allowing Maya to assimilate this new experience.

"Next, imagine the light radiating from within you. Shining out past the bubble barrier and into the world." Michael pauses for a few moments, allowing Maya to sink into the experience.

"Now bring this expansive energy back into your bubble and keep it contained within your six-foot bubble … Now, while you sit in this blissful energy, I want you to listen to your surroundings … not only the children laughing over at the playground, but also the tiniest sounds … like a cricket, or an ant crawling on your blanket."

"How do you know that?" Maya stops the meditation with this all-encompassing question.

"Actually, I don't," answers Michael. "I just assumed that because you're in a park, on your blanket, there is likely an anthill nearby. There must be some scavengers searching for your snacks!

"In the past, I would have been able to sense everything around you, but since the Pruner destroyed my internal clock, I sense nothing. You are the first person that I have been able to contact … and even that is beyond expectation. Our internal clocks are what allow us to interact. It's really quite unfathomable that we've been able to connect. I have been sitting here for months putting forth the energy that I would be able to communicate with someone without my internal clock, not knowing if it would work. This is truly a miracle!"

"Whoa! The Pruner? What exactly happened? Are you okay?" Maya asks, concerned.

"Oh Maya, I'm sorry … It's a lot of information," Michael responds. "Let's explore each of those questions more as you learn."

Maya sits still for a moment.

"So, I guess you are pretty glad I said yes!" she chuckles.

"You wouldn't believe how happy I am!" he smiles.

"Does this mean that one day I will be able to sense the things that are going on around me *and* the people that I communicate with?" Maya wonders.

"I hope so!" Michael says.

"Cool!" she beams.

"Okay, let's refocus," Michael redirects.

"Yes, sorry for the distraction," Maya apologizes.

"No worries, it's good for you to understand," he says.

For the greater part of an hour, Maya practises sensing her space again, with Michael's guidance, before he says, "Right, you should go for a quick walk and have your snack. Next, we are going to try something different."

GROUNDING

MAYA TAKES A quick walk around the park to stretch her legs and eat her granola bar. When she returns, Michael starts explaining before she sits down.

"You are doing great, Maya!" Michael encourages. "For this, we need to change positions for the first few times. Move yourself over to a bench. I want you to sit upright with your feet flat on the ground and about shoulder-width apart." Maya turns and walks back toward the bench she had just passed.

"Great," Michael continues. "You will close your eyes again and—"

"Will my eyes always be closed?" Maya questions, a bit frustrated.

"Good question. No. It is just easier to learn with your eyes closed so that you don't get distracted by your surroundings. Once you start mastering your skills, you will most likely be able to open your eyes and connect easily on the move."

"Okay, great!" Maya looks off into the distance and adds, "I'm looking forward to that!"

"Where was I?" Michael mumbles. "Oh yes … with your eyes closed, I want you to imagine a ball of white light at your heart centre."

"My what?" Maya queries.

"Your heart centre, or heart chakra. Have you not heard about chakras before?" probes Michael.

"Oh, yeah, I guess so. I've heard my mom talking about them a bit. I think there are seven, right?" Maya expands, "And they each have a colour and meaning. Oh, and my mom often chants something different with each one as well."

Michael smiles. "Yes, there are seven common chakras, moving from your hips up to the crown of your head. They do each have a colour and many positive mantras. Plus, they each have a seed sound which is likely what you hear your mom chanting. They also each connect to different areas of the body and healing. We will definitely learn a lot more about them, but for today, you only need the basics.

"So, your heart chakra is essentially the place in your chest where your heart is. Think of it like a small circle, or a spinning wheel, just beneath the surface of your ribs where your heart is," he describes.

"Like here?" Maya touches her chest.

"Exactly!" Michael exclaims. "Now, to help you visualize, think of your hips, or the base of your seat, as the root chakra. This is where you ground to Mother Earth. Next is the sacral chakra, located beneath your belly button. Third is the solar plexus, fourth is the heart chakra, fifth is the throat chakra, sixth is the third eye chakra, located in your forehead, and lastly is the crown chakra, at the top of your head, connecting you up to Source Energy."

Maya takes a moment to review. "Root, sacral, solar plexus, heart, throat, third eye, crown. Rest so sweetly here throughout thine connection."

"Huh?" Michael wonders.

"Oh," Maya giggles, "I'm not great at remembering things so I make up little phrases to remind me of the order. It a mnemonic device."

"Alright!" Michael grins., "Whatever works for you— 'Rest so sweetly here throughout thine connection,' it is!"

"Thank you," Maya replies.

"Let's begin," Michael starts again. "Imagine a ball of white light and tell me when you have it."

"It's there. I have it," Maya answers.

"Awesome! I want you to visualize that white light as a ball of loving energy." Michael pauses. "If it helps, envision someone you love."

"Like my mom?" she asks.

"Sure! Mom, dad, grandma, grandpa, sister, brother, anyone!" Michael adds.

"Cool! Okay, I see her," says Maya.

"It is cool, but it is only the first step in grounding," Michael explains.

"Grounding?" inquires Maya. "You mentioned that when you brought up the root chakra. What is that?"

"Grounding is the process of connecting to the earth. Think of it like the roots of a tree. Your roots are just as expansive into the ground. You will visualize your hips and legs branching off into the earth to ground all of your energy to this place. Conversely, connecting to Source Energy is sort of like connecting to the channel of light from you in this physical space on earth up into the sky. It is very important." Michael pauses and watches Maya for her reaction. When she nods, he continues.

"Close your eyes. We're going to start with the bubble exercise and move on from there. Inhale, exhale—sigh it out. Inhale, and on your next exhale, I want you to envision the ball of white light at your heart centre, expanding with your breath. Breathe into your heart centre. Think of your mom and make this ball as bright as your love for your mom. Now, expand this love for your mom into bubble. Imagine this bright golden light, and then with your next exhale, breathe it out to the whole world. Do this pattern three more times, inhale radiating light and love, exhale sending it out to the universe, across all times and spaces.

"Inhale, and on your next exhale imagine this ball of light energy travelling down from your heart centre, through your lower three chakras, through your solar plexus, through your sacral chakra, and finally through your root chakra. Imagine this energy moving through your hips and legs and out your feet, into the ground, travelling deep into the earth's core, into the centre of Mother Earth. Then, once you get there, inhale and retrace the path back up, bringing the white light back to your feet and up into your heart centre. All of this happens within a split second … in the time it takes to breathe in and out.

"Now on the next exhale, you are going to breath this loving ball of light up through the three upper chakras, up through the throat chakra, up through the third eye and finally up and out of the crown chakra at the top of your head. Visualize a larger ball of light above you in the sky, far out in the sky or universe. Imagine your light connecting up to this giant circular light in the sky, this powerful Source Energy. Imagine the light between your energy and Source Energy creating a solid beam or channel for light to travel on, allowing you to connect more deeply to Source and to your higher self and the Collective Consciousness that resides around us.

"Then, in a split second, inhale and follow this energy as it returns down to your heart chakra, bringing more white light and healing energy through this beam down into your heart centre. This combined process is connecting and grounding, and I want you to practise it for the next five minutes, and then we'll talk about it."

After five minutes, Michael takes a deep inhale and exhales a sigh to enter into Maya's consciousness.

"Okay Maya," Michael soothes, "Take a deep inhale, and allow your next exhale to release a giant sigh. Now, bring your awareness back to your body. Keep your eyes closed, start to wiggle your fingers and toes … begin listening to your surroundings … awaken some movement in your neck, completing some gentle neck rolls. Inhale, shrug your shoulders and exhale, roll them down your back … and when you feel ready, open your eyes."

Maya slowly completes each instruction. As she opens her eyes, she stretches and yawns. Bringing her hands to her eyes, she rubs under and over her occipital bone. She takes a deep breath and looks out to the park.

"What did you think?" Michael asks.

Maya takes a deep breath and nods.

"Wow! That was amazing." Then Maya expands, "The energy seems to start so small; I couldn't imagine where this exercise was going, but then it was as if the energy was getting more and more powerful each time I breathed through a cycle!"

"Exactly. It is such a powerful tool to help you connect each day! I often meditate using this tool alone. However, there are more tools you will need to help you be successful on your journey. Remember to practise this every day until you begin your journey."

"I can definitely do that. How long should I do it each day?" asks Maya.

"Five minutes a day is good. You can increase from there as you feel ready. Or you could do five minutes in the morning and five minutes at night," guides Michael. "The next step though, is really going to blow you away!"

"Awesome! Let me just do a quick stretch." Maya stands up and reaches for the sky. She walks back to her blanket and does a few stretches before sitting down again.

TOYING
WITH TIME

"THIS NEXT STEP can be tricky and a little danger-ous," Michael begins, "so I am going to give you some ground rules."

"Okay." Maya waits.

"When you start to move into various time-space reali-ties it is imperative, in the beginning, that I know exactly the moment in time where you are going or I don't think I will be able to contact you," Michael explains. "So, initially, I will need you to describe the key elements of where you want to visit. Second, we need to start by visiting a spe-cific situation in your past to ensure that you are travel-ling accurately and safely, understanding the concept and ensuring that you will be able to return to this moment safely as well."

"Definitely! So, what do I need to do?" Maya asks.

"Well, for starters," Michael says, "I need you to open your eyes and note the surroundings of the park, and tell me all of the details and the exact time and date today."

Maya surveys the park. "The park is really designed for family use. As you walk up the main path there are four benches, two on each side, facing in. On your right is an area for younger children. There are logs to climb on, springy fish for children to rock on, a disc swing, a baby swing, and one of those accessible swings where a wheelchair can roll right onto. The whole area is in the shape of a turtle with fabricated stones as the head and legs. There is an adult workout station around the outer edges of this part of the park.

"On the opposite side of the path is a skateboard park and a pickleball court. As you walk farther along the path there is a splash pad and a service building. There are two picnic tables there. Past the building is the zipline and giant slides set within the forested area. I like to hang out in the tunnel over there. That's where I first heard you … Right now, I am sitting on the mound between the pickleball court and the zipline. It is May seventh, 2022. The time is ten fifty-four a.m."

"Wow. That's an amazing park! Look around and see if there is something in particular that is a little unusual that you will remember when you get back," Michael instructs. "It may be a person or a specific animal—something like that."

Maya looks around again, for something out of the ordinary. "There is a baby here with dark brown curls, wearing a striped hat."

"Okay great, Maya. Look at him again. Tell me the details of his clothing, including the colours of the striped hat," Michael pushes.

Maya looks at the baby and starts describing him. "He's sitting in a stroller. His dad is pushing him while his mom is chatting to him. He is wearing little khaki pants with elastic on the bottom. His shoes are more like slippers, navy blue on top with the face of a seal, and grey leather on the bottom. He has what looks like a white T-shirt or onesie underneath his navy thin-knitted sweater. It has an angled collar with a button on the right-hand side. My right ... when I am looking at him. His hat is made of cotton. It is different shades of blue, five in all, with beige stripes between each blue stripe. It starts with navy at the bottom and moves up to a baby blue. There is the tiniest pompom on top."

"Excellent!" Michael congratulates her. "This is the sort of details you will need to remember when shifting. If any detail is different, it could signify that you need to shift again to the correct time-space reality. Also, you need to remember the date and time in this space for when you want to come back. You need to reinsert yourself into the exact moment you leave so that no one here notices you were ever gone. Just before we begin, we will check the time again to be more accurate."

"Okay, what's next?" Maya asks.

"You need to pick an event that is extremely clear in your mind that we can go back to visit. It needs to be an event that you can verify if you were able to find it correctly. Does that make sense?" checks Michael.

"Find it correctly? I'm confused, how can an event change?" clarifies Maya.

"That's a great question," Michael pauses, "but honestly, that is far more information than you need right now and we don't really have the time to go into great detail. What I can tell you is that we live in a variety of dimensions based on vibrations. You will have to trust me that there are alternate time-space realities. What you do need to realize is, if for any reason you think something feels off, shift back to this time-space reality immediately. Don't worry about anything else—just get back here."

"Okay, sounds good," Maya concedes, "but I definitely want to hear about them at some point!"

"I promise you will! Have you chosen an event?" Michael asks.

"Yes! My seventh birthday party!" Maya beams.

"Great! What makes your seventh birthday party so memorable?" asks Michael. "And be very clear."

"Well for starters, I guess, it was all about me!" Maya giggles. "My mom went all out! All of my friends were invited with their parents. It was a pool party for the kids. It was a mid-year, six-month party … sort of Christmas in June idea, since my birthday is in December and no one can ever come to my party. It was actually my seventh and a half birthday! There was a clown and a bouncy castle. The clown was a bit juvenile but at least no one was scared of him and the castle was a blast for all ages! I think the adults had more fun bouncing in it than the kids! We had cupcakes rather than a cake. They were blue and white. The cupcakes had either bright blue icing with a white chocolate dot in the middle or white icing with a dark blue dot in the centre. They were delicious. I remember at the time, I wanted to eat like five of them. I did get one of each though, so that was cool! My best friend from when

I was little was there. Sally. She was great. We did everything together until her family moved away.

"For lunch, we ate hotdogs and hamburgers off the barbecue. There were tons of different types of salads and chips. Everything was so yummy."

"Awesome! You're making my mouth water! I can't wait to see!" says Michael. "Can you remember the exact date and time of the party?"

"It was June twenty-fourth, 2016," Maya said confidently. "Almost exactly six months after my seventh birthday and from my eighth birthday. I had never celebrated a six-month party before. It was so cool to have everyone wish me happy birthday and pretend it was December! It was a Saturday, and the party went from one to four p.m."

"Okay, let's both think of June twenty-fourth, 2016, at two twenty-two," says Michael. "That will insert us into the party when there are already guests there."

"Are you going to be there?" questions Maya.

"I think so; in your mind. I'm going to try at least! I can't physically travel at this point in time, but I'm hoping to tag onto your energy," says Michael, sounding sad. "If for some reason I am wrong, check out the scene to make sure it is just as you remember and then think of this exact moment to come back to."

"Right … what happens if someone sees me?" wonders Maya.

"There aren't actually any issues with running into your old self at this point," Michael responds, "or people who know you. That second part can be tricky, but at this point in time, people won't really recognize you, as you're much older. They might comment on the similarities though. If they ask you who you are, just tell them you were a lunch helper in Maya's classroom before you moved to the middle school. Then make sure to get distracted by something and rush off. Oh, and make up a fake name just in case."

"Oh, okay," Maya pauses. "I thought that when you time travel that you can't see yourself or it warps reality."

"That sounds like a movie," laughs Michael. "It's not true. I talk to myself all the time!"

"Cool! Is there anything I should say to my younger self?" Maya asks.

"No. I wouldn't even try to talk to yourself. Not yet. Let's just get through training and we can worry about the fun stuff later," Michael continues.

"Okay," shrugs Maya, "I get it."

"Tell me again, what's the date and exact time right now, and is the baby still there?" Michael asks.

"Yes, he is," says Maya, "and it's May seventh, 2022, at eleven-eleven a.m."

"Excellent," says Michael. "Do not forget. May seventh, 2022, at eleven-eleven a.m."

"Got it!" confirms Maya.

"Let's do it!" Michael nearly shouts. "I'll walk you through your initial grounding, then I'll try to follow you to the party."

"Perfect," says Maya.

"Close your eyes and start by taking three deep inhales with giant sighs when you exhale, then balance your breathing to normal," Michael begins. "When you feel relaxed, create the ball of white light at your heart centre. Visualize it growing to encompass your body and your bubble. Now on each inhale, visualize your bubble getting bigger and brighter, and on each exhale, visualize it travelling down through your feet to Mother Earth and back up through your heart centre and up through your head to Source Energy. Continue with this process until you are ready. Then, think of your party. Think of June twenty-fourth, 2016, at two twenty-two p.m. See you soon!"

BIRTHDAY

'WOW! THIS IS big!' Maya thinks as she arrives at the party. She had forgotten just how big the party had felt at that moment. She touches some streamers as she walks through the hallway toward the outdoor patio. It is very noisy. There is a clown in the living room. The kitchen island is full of food, the side tables hold a bunch of glasses and a variety of drinks. Maya hears squeals of joy and splashing outside. She peers out the kitchen window and sees her friends doing cannonballs into the pool.

'Aw … It was so much fun!' Maya reminisces.

"Maya! Maya! Do you hear me?" Michael calls.

"Hey! Yes! I totally forgot what was happening! How strange is this?" answers Maya.

"Totally! The first time is always the strangest!" Michael agrees. "Take a look around. Do you see anything out of place, or is everything the same?"

Maya looks around the room. "Everything is the same, I think!"

"Maya, you need to be sure," Michael says seriously. "Any small detail can mean danger. Look at everything! Take a quick walk around and double-check."

Maya walks around the kitchen island and outside to the pool area. She scans the guests, noting her friends and family who have come to celebrate with her. Everyone looks so young. She notices Charlie, their old black and white cocker spaniel curled up under the swinging bench. Charlie perks his ears up and lifts his head to look at her. She bends down to pet his head. "Hi Charlie, I've missed you! You could never be fooled!" Charlie licks Maya's hand and turns, almost confused to look at the younger version of her. Maya notices his gaze, scratches behind his right ear, and quickly walks around the party.

"Yup, Michael, everything looks the same."

"Perfect!" Michael says. "Come on back!"

"Come on back?" Maya questions.

"Yes," Michael responds. "We've got work to do! Remember, come back to your original date. Don't forget to ground yourself through your white light heart centre first and then connect the pillar of light down through Mother Earth's core and up to Source Energy."

"On it! See you on the flip side!" Maya walks back into the house and sneaks into her old room for a moment of quiet. She briefly looks at the pictures on the walls and the trinkets on her desk, remembering this time of her life fondly. She touches a small mood ring and promises herself to try to find it back in her own time-space reality. She goes to sit on the bed. She closes her eyes and starts to ground.

ॐ

"Wow!" Maya exclaims once she had come back into her body awareness in her own time-space reality. "That was like nothing I have ever experienced before! How is that possible? How do more people not know about this?"

"It's an awakening, Maya!" Michael explains. "More people are connecting. They are learning how to meditate and tune in to the frequency of the universe. It's happening! People are waking up to their potential!

"But not everyone is happy about that. This is exactly what the Pruner is fighting. We don't know all of his reasoning yet, but we need to work fast to ensure that this freedom continues to be available to everyone. It's a tricky situation on many levels. People are able to learn this skill as they are developmentally ready to awaken, *or* as they are taken in by a mentor. It's a skill that is useful to be learned within certain parameters and responsibilities. Unfortunately, if we are unsuccessful, our cause will be put back hundreds of years and the face of humanity will change drastically."

GRAVITY

MAYA WALKS HOME slowly, thinking about the gravity of the situation. If she is unsuccessful, humanity will change forever. That's a lot for a thirteen-year-old. It's literally the weight of the world.

When she gets home, Maya goes directly to see her mom in the living room. She is reading, of course.

"Hey Mom! How's it going?" calls Maya.

"Great love, you?" she holds up a finger, meaning Maya needs to wait until she finishes that sentence or paragraph. Then she looks up expectantly.

"I am pretty good," Maya pauses. "I have a question, a sort of hypothetical assignment for homework. Can I give you a basic outline and you can talk me through it and try to give me some advice?"

"Well, I don't know if I will be of any help, but I sure can try!" Mom laughs.

"Thanks, Mom," Maya begins "Imagine there was a problem, a big ethical problem, and you were asked to help in some way. It's dangerous, but without your help, many people could die. What do you do?"

"Hmm," responds Mom, "could people die even if you do help?"

"Potentially." Maya confirms.

"But people will definitely die if you don't help."

"Yes." answers Maya.

"Could you die?" Mom looks at Maya imploringly.

"I guess so." she shrugs.

"Ooh, that's tough." Mom waits. "The mom in me says no way … but the ethical part of me says you should still try if you had a good chance of saving people. Maybe the question you need to ask your teacher is, what are the odds?"

"The odds." Maya nods, "Yes, I need more details about the odds." Maya pauses. "Thanks, Mom! One more question. You have been asked to save the world. If you do, you risk your life and the lives of the people you love, but if you don't, life as you know it may not continue to exist. What do you do?"

"Oh, that's a much easier one." Mom giggles.

Maya scrunches her face. "It is?"

"Yes … of course, you save the world. If you don't, you won't have anywhere to live anyway. And bonus points for becoming a superhero! Super Maya!" Mom laughs and sticks her hand in the air like Superman, then she pulls Maya in for a hug.

"A superhero. Right. Cool. Thanks." Maya laughs nervously and stands up, ready to walk away.

"Cool project! I'd love to hear more of these either/or questions!" Mom says.

"I'll keep that in mind, Mom. I'm going to go tinker in the basement." Maya heads downstairs for the rest of the evening, psyching herself up to become a modern day superhero.

IN TUNE

ON SUNDAY MORNING, Maya rushes back to the park for another day of training. She is exhausted and sore from sitting still all day, but she is excited to soak up more lessons.

"Good morning, Michael! I'm here!" connects Maya.

"Good morning, Maya! Did you have a good night?" asks Michael.

"Pretty good. I was exhausted, but I slept well." Maya answers.

"You will find that when you start meditating and shifting, you can feel tired from learning so much new material and from sitting in the same position for so long. The best way to minimize exhaustion is to do some light stretching, like yoga, and set the intention when you are expanding your white light to energize or re-energize yourself first before taking the next step." explains Michael. "Does that make sense?"

"Yes, completely." Maya nods. "Fill myself first. Like the saying, fill your own cup first. Will do."

"Awesome, how are you feeling about jumping in today?" asks Michael.

"Good. It's a lot to take in, but I feel ready to dive deeper!" Maya answers honestly.

"Amazing! Let's get started. We still have three main things that you will need to be able to do." Michael says. "One, you need to learn how to communicate with others. Two, set up blocks. And three, travel fast without being found.

"Travelling to unknown places is the starting place. You need to start some research to prepare yourself for travelling to places you don't know anything about or have never visited. To do that, you will need a library or a device. Are you close to a library? Or do you have a device?"

"I have a tablet." Maya replies, "But I need to be connected. There's a library down the road. Would that be a better choice?"

"Yes." answers Michael, "That's perfect because we will have more options. Sometimes it's nice to look through books rather than a tablet. Try walking to the library while chatting with me. If it doesn't work and you lose contact with me, reconnect once you get there."

"Okay," Maya thinks as she packs up her things, "can you tell me something new or pertinent while I'm walking?"

"Yes, for sure, Michael answers. "My brother, who I mentioned, can connect anywhere … any moment … while doing anything. It's truly amazing. It can take years of practice to master. He is just always connected and in tune. It totally blows my mind. I'm hoping you are one of those people. I have to specifically sit down, calm myself and connect to be in tune, but some people are always in tune and they just need to check in with their higher self or the Collective rather than reconnecting each time."

"Very cool! What do I need to do to practice that?" asks Maya.

"There are many parts to the whole process." responds Michael. "We'll start with heading to the library and see how the connection goes."

"I'm almost at the library!" says Maya.

"What? No way!" exclaims Michael.

"Yeah! It's only a couple blocks away from the park." laughs Maya. "You said you were going to tell me a story while I walked here."

"I did. But … There was no chatter. No interruptions," Michael replies incredulously.

"No chatter? No interruptions?" repeats Maya.

"I didn't think it would be that good of a connection—if any connection at all. I heard you loud and clear the whole time you were walking. Normally there would be a fuzzy connection at some point. A fuzz, like static … think of when your TV or radio is static … that sort of thing. And interruptions are like a loud noise or a blip where you lose sound for a second. Talking to you, there was nothing; it was perfectly clear. This is amazing! It means you ARE!" shouts Michael.

"I am what?" Maya wonders.

"You are in tune! Like all the time! You've dialed into the frequency … You can likely communicate ALL THE TIME. Unless it is just with me, which I highly doubt. This is so freaking amazing!"

THE PRUNER

"THE FIRST THING you need to do is research ten …" Michael pauses, "a minimum of ten places in time. These will be places you can visit if you need to when making the Mayday call. You will also travel to each of these locations to practice shifting to different time-space realities. Think of them like emergency drop zones that the Clippers don't know about and would need to spend time trying to figure out where you are hiding. You will need to find some facts, images, dates, and times that you can visit. You will also want to know if there is a specific time that you shouldn't visit. For instance, I do not recommend visiting during war-torn periods of time. It can add a layer of danger that we don't need right now.

"So … treat this like a school assignment. Pretend you are planning a vacation and you need to know every detail of your trip before you leave. As you are finding this information, begin to visualize what it would look like for you to be in these spaces."

"Okay, question," Maya interjects. "I am not actually going to travel to these places?"

"Soon," Michael responds. "Once you have your list and share your research with me, I will try to meet you in a few of those places. Then we will try a different type of travel, once you are ready to broadcast the Mayday message, you will need to tap into the Collective energy, which I don't want you doing from your time-space reality. It's too dangerous. Travelling will allow your home and your family a greater sense of safety. If the Clippers start to track you, you don't want them coming here. Plus, you will need to have random locations that you can shift to in order to throw off their scent of you—so to speak … in tracking terms."

"How exactly do they track?" wonders Maya.

"That's the thing … once you are connected to Source Energy, you realize and truly understand that we are all connected. We are all one. We can all sense each other." Michael waits for Maya to acknowledge that she understands. Once she nods, he continues, "For that reason, the second thing you need to learn is how to set up blocks. Normally, it is okay to have the Collective know where you are. Normally, we are all contentedly connected and if someone needs us, we want them to be able to find us. However, if ever you need to disconnect from being found you can shut off your connection completely for a short time. Everything we do is about intention, so while we usually have faith that all is good and safe, it is imperative to be extra cautious on this journey.

"Disconnecting can be as simple as envisioning a black tarp, blanket, or sheath over your whole bubble. But this can become a very dark place. You need to remember to lift the blackness as soon as you are done with the disconnection, or it can wreak havoc on your daily emotional state and interactions with others. Disconnecting is both easier and more drastic than blocking. It is only to be used when absolutely necessary.

"Blocking, on the other hand, is a technique that allows you to continue your connection to Source Energy, but cancels the transmission to certain beings within the Collective. It's more in depth to set up because you have to put out the intention to block specific members of the Collective. The problem we are facing with the Clippers is that we don't know how they are getting past the blocks to track us. At this point, we can only do what we know works so far."

"Why is it that the Pruner, a man so impure, has access to such a pure form of energy?" asks Maya.

"Ooh, great question Maya!" Michael starts, "He wasn't always this way. His life was quite blessed. He was a farmer with a beautiful family. He connected to Source Energy early in life, and discovered new ways to farm that honoured the earth and the cycles of the seasons. These methods also yielded large amounts of produce to serve the growing masses. He was known as a true visionary. He was able to connect many people through meditation to the Collective and raise the vibration of the planet. Many more people began to understand how to shift because of his contributions and we are grateful to him for that."

"Oh wow! So, what happened that changed?" probes Maya.

"Apparently, he became overwhelmed by the power that he had discovered, and he started craving more recognition," Michael explains. "In the beginning, when the farmer was introducing so many new people to their inherent connection, the Collective valued his contributions. However, the Collective works on the ideal that we are all created equal. We *all* have a contribution to make to the Collective. We each have a gift—a service to offer to the Collective once we are ready to shine. Each person's growth has its divine time and place for their leadership to flow through. There is not one leader. It's actually a universal law required for the greater good. All beings contribute to their highest purpose and the highest good of the Collective."

"One second, sorry to interrupt." Maya interjects while slightly raising her hand, then noticing and giggling at her action, "What are universal laws?"

"Universal laws are the laws of nature, Michael explains. "They are the things that always hold true, regardless of circumstance. There are debates over how many universal laws exist, but most people believe there are twelve. For instance, the law of oneness, the law of vibration, the law of cause and effect, and the law of attraction. Regardless of the number of laws, by understanding these laws, we can better make decisions about how we authentically show up in the world. Honestly, learning about universal laws is one of the coolest processes in life—but there is far too many details to cover at this time. Can we come back to this at a later date?"

"Yes of course; I'm sorry." apologizes Maya.

"No worries, but if you haven't noticed, I can get distracted and go on tangents as well. I am so passionate about all of this, but we have important things to get to first!" Michael urges.

Maya nods.

"Anyway, when new leaders were starting to contribute and rise into their own power," Michael continues, "the farmer initially tried to control the flow of information—inserting himself and his views into the process, building up his self-importance, and trying to make other members feel like their contributions were less important. This indirectly devalued their self-worth and their innate ability to share their light. The farmer's ego started driving his decisions, rather than tapping into his higher self and his connection to Source Energy.

"As members became wiser and were willing to gently challenge the farmer's hierarchy, he struggled with releasing control. The farmer took the transfer of leadership quite hard because he felt he was losing followers and losing his influence. He became less and less supportive of new ideas and rising stars. The farmer tried to place rules and parameters on the Collective which would keep him in a position more revered as a powerful contributor. In the long run, these notions of power and control could not be upheld by universal laws. More and more people began to realize that the farmer was trying to overstep his limits.

"Eventually, we held a Collective hearing in which we decided as a whole that as a consequence of exerting power over the Collective, the farmer would need to relinquish his leadership role, and he was banned from shifting for a whole year.

"As a group, we were able to put in place a powerful meditation that forced the farmer to forget his knowledge of the Collective and his understanding of how to shift.

"All of his family and friends were part of this Collective agreement. We thought the disconnect would allow the farmer to reconnect to his roots, re-charge and re-centre on his own life and his own loving surroundings. We stayed in contact with his family throughout the year, but it seemed to get worse over time. The more disconnected he felt throughout the year, the more anger he housed in his heart. He became bitter and mean. When his sentence was up and he remembered who he had been and what had been done to him, he became irate and inconsolable. His family said that he became a recluse and disowned them.

"From what we understand now, he had taken that time to create a vicious tool that would jab into a person's heart centre and remove their internal clock, keeping them from ever shifting and likely communicating with the Collective again."

"So, if he was a recluse, and the Collective had essentially banished him, how did he recruit all of the Clippers?" Maya questions.

"Another good question, Maya!" Michael congratulates, "The farmer had a few loyal allies that continued to make contact with him, and they chose to leave the Collective, but most of the Clippers, from what we understand, are new trainees. The farmer shifted around the world recruiting nefarious folks whom he blackmailed into working for him. He first taught them they had an internal clock and then threatened to remove it. These are the types of people who wouldn't likely learn about their internal clock on their own—so they are excited to learn this skill that can take them to new worlds that they can pilfer and then disappear. Plus, they are also less likely to worry about the collective good, or doing the right thing as they are not yet this evolved.

"This is where the problem lies moving forward. Once we take down the Pruner, we will need to actively train the Clippers or else there will be all sorts of confusion in each time-space reality as the Clippers try to reintegrate into their lives and potentially train shifters who don't have any collective responsibility."

"Oh, that does sound dangerous. When did people started calling the farmer, the Pruner?" asks Maya.

"We think it was his own doing, actually." suggests Michael. "We think he started calling himself that to the Clippers as he recruited them. A play on his former career … instead of farming the land, he was looking to prune humanity."

"Whoa. That's sinister." comments Maya.

"Definitely. You do not want to get caught by him or his Clippers." notes Michael. "But I don't want you to worry about that too much. I want you to stay focused on the positive. You will have a message to deliver to the masses. You will be successful—I can feel it!"

"That's very reassuring, Michael." says Maya, with a slight tone of hesitancy.

PROTECTION

MAYA TRIES TO focus on her research. She is up to five locations, when she says, "Michael, I don't understand how knowing the location of historical places and times will save me."

"Once you open yourself up as a portal for connective energy, the Pruner and his Clippers will sense you and start to search for you. You will need to be very careful. I need to teach you enough basics to warn the others, while at the same time providing you with the tools to both protect yourself and your family, as well as have a getaway plan if needed." Michael answers.

"Yes. Let's start there. How do I protect my family?" asks Maya.

"For starters, once we begin this mission and you leave this time-space reality, you'll need to forget about it for a long time." says Michael. "You'll reinsert yourself at some point in time when it's safer, but in order to keep your family safe you *must not* come back to this time-space reality. You must try not to think ... no, that's not a strong enough statement ... you MUST NOT think about your family. It's very dangerous."

"Okay, is there any other way to protect them?" Maya asks.

"It's really those two things that we have talked about. Don't shift to or from your time-space reality once it starts, and do not think about your family or this time-space reality. That's it. It sounds simple, but it is actually quite hard to do, especially if you are lonely." Michael says, sounding sad.

"Okay. I will keep that in mind. Michael, I'm sorry you're lonely." consoles Maya.

"Thank you, Maya. It is definitely the hardest thing that has ever happened to me. Luckily, I have you to talk to now—it helps." Michael laments.

"So, to ensure you don't end up in the same situation as me—in order to protect yourself, you will need to be able to shift time-space realities quickly and without being caught. Luckily, you will not need to sit down to connect because you are in tune all of the time. You will be able to walk or run around in a time-space reality and shift to the next time-space reality while moving.

"Once you have your ten researched places, I will feel safer about moving forward. Also, once you have the first ten places, you will research ten more places that I don't know about. That way, if my position is compromised, I won't know your escape route. Truthfully, I don't think I could bare knowing they caught you. I feel like I've already been tortured beyond anything else they could do to me, but just to be safe, it's an added measure.

"Then, we will pick a few places to go and practice, but they must be far away from your emergency drop zones. I can try to meet you there once you begin your journey. I also want to teach you the Mayday message before we begin so that you can practice. Worst case scenario—you will know it—if you have to start broadcasting before we planned. You might only get one chance."

"Whoa! Whoa! That was a lot of information. You said like five important things there. Compromised? You think our connection might get compromised?" implores Maya.

"Truthfully, I'm not sure … but in my experience," Michael pauses, "evil always has a backup plan, so it's better to be overprepared and go in super positive with our own plans so that we feel super confident in our efforts."

"Right. Sounds good. So, I research ten places that we will talk about … and then I research ten more places that I don't tell you about," Maya reiterates. "Is that correct?"

Michael nods. "Yes, that's technically it, but you'll need a bit more attention to detail. You'll need to be very specific. Remember when you travelled to your birthday and you needed a lot of details to ensure it was accurate? Travelling to unknown time-space realities is more difficult because you won't always know if it is the truest version of that time-space reality or a trap designed to fool you. You will need to do a lot of research, and you will also need to trust your intuition. If there is any inkling that something is off when you arrive somewhere, don't risk it, shift to a new location immediately."

"What happens if I end up in a false reality?" queries Maya.

"As I mentioned, it is likely a trap. You'll need to move quickly to a new time-space reality." explains Michael. "It's not worth the risk to stick around to find out. You'll need to move lightning fast—within seconds—to a new time-space reality. It is better to evade the Clippers from the beginning, but if they do link onto your frequency, they will come for you very quickly, and you will need to try to lose them quickly and get refocused to make the Mayday call."

"Wait a minute," Maya puts both her hands up. "These are the people who caught you? I need to be better than YOU? Isn't that impossible? You're amazing!!"

"Well, truthfully, I'm hoping you are much better than me." Michael blushes. "I may have more experience, but you are in tune. It will definitely help you. I've never heard of anyone learning quite as quickly as you to maintain contact while not sitting grounded. This is mind-blowing—you have learned so fast!"

"Well, isn't that because you're an awesome teacher?" Maya says with a smile.

Michael laughs. "Let's not worry about that … and be awesome together!"

"Right. Sorry. Sidetracked. Clearly, I have the same problem as you—going on tangents." Maya notices. "So, once I go to these places … I'll revisit them?"

"Sort of," Michael starts. "Once you find the ten places that you are going to share with me, you will travel to them and I will try to meet you in a couple of them. Then, once we're sure you are travelling well, I will explain how to travel to unknown destinations and to set up blocks. Then, you can take some time to think, process and memorize all of this information.

"If I am able to meet up with you, I also want us to practice having you set up blocks before I come meet you. But that's getting ahead of ourselves. Finish the research and let's go from there."

"Okay, but if I am setting up blocks, isn't that dangerous? Couldn't the Clippers find me at the same time?" worries Maya.

"True, but the Clippers are searching for an alert frequency," explains Michael. "We should be okay with general travel until you broadcast the Mayday message. While you are shifting between places, you need to be very careful not to think about connecting or alerting the Community. That's very important. You will need to keep your mind clear. We are doing this specifically so that you can practice.

"Think about it … can you hide your thoughts from me? Your friend? Maybe, but not likely—yet. The Clippers have tools to breathe into your thoughts. You need to be hyper-vigilant at covering your thoughts, and this might allow you to see how quickly someone in the Community can find you so that you are better prepared. I cannot stress enough the importance of a clear mind. It could be devastating. We do need to practice, but we are not ready for that kind of exposure yet. Clear?"

"Clear." Maya repeats.

"Okay Maya, take the rest of your time today to finish researching your emergency drops and travel locations." says Michael. "Remember to include exact times and locations, down to the minute. The last thing you want is to end up shifting into an area of conflict. Be sure to choose safe situations to minimize danger … but also, choose locations that aren't too secluded. Seclusion can also prove very dangerous. When you are done, give me a call and we can talk about the ten planned visits."

"Okay, sounds good. Chat soon." replies Maya.

TRAVEL AGENT

AFTER COMPLETING HER research, Maya returns to the park and contacts Michael.

"Michael. Michael! Can you hear me?"

"Yes! I've been waiting for you!" smiles Michael. "It's a little boring over here!"

"No doubt. Okay, I've got my twenty locations … let's talk about the first ten." says Maya.

"Perfect!" Michael responds. "I can't wait to hear about them."

Maya runs through her research list, noting the key events on each day that she can check to verify the time.

MAYA'S RESEARCH - TO SHARE WITH MICHAEL

• Walt Disney World, October 1, 1982, 10:15 a.m. The opening of the Epcot Centre. They released 15,000 balloons. Meet in front of the stage where the dancers are all in white and the band is in blue.
• Peaceful COVID protest in London, England, April 20, 2020, 12:20 p.m. Meet in front of Buckingham Palace next to the guard house. Protesters will be walking the streets, some with masks, which might make a good cover! Wait to the right of the guard house.
• NASA's Space Shuttle Launch July 8, 2011, 11:29 a.m. Meet in front of the large clock with 13 seconds remaining.
• Calgary Stampede July 10, 1950, 6:30 p.m. Meet under the sign for the CFAC building.
• Eiffel Tower March 31, 1889, 3:33 p.m. Meet at the base on the north leg.
• Summer Olympics in Mexico, October 12, 1968, 10:30 a.m. Meet at the base of the stairs leading up to the flame.
• Sydney Opera House October 20, 1973, 4:53 p.m. Meet at the base of the first flag pole to the left of the main entryway.

- Sensō-ji Temple, Japan, June 6, 1912, 8:15 a.m.
  Meet just inside the gate in front of the first booth on the right.

- Palolem Beach, South Goa, January 14, 2000, 3:15 p.m.
  Meet in front of the yellow wooden hut called Dreams of Palolem.

- Great Wall of China May 13, 1975, 10:05 a.m.
  Meet in Jinshanling at the topmost building near the rounded door on the east side.

"Wow! Those sound great, Maya!" Michael praises. "Let's keep up the pace; we have one more thing to practice before we come back to the idea of travel."

BLOCKS

"I BRIEFLY TOUCHED on the idea of blocks, but we got distracted." laughs Michael. "You need to be able to set up blocks for the Pruner, his Clippers, and anyone who might be loyal to his cause."

"Oh right, you started to explain it and I asked another question." giggles Maya.

"Exactly." chuckles Michael. "Anyway, setting up blocks is simple in and of itself, but it requires greater caution and focus than simply disconnecting. In addition, you're going to try to set up a block for the whole Community, so that the Pruner and his supporters can't decipher our plan through connecting with other Community members.

"When you start to ground yourself, you need to set very clear intentions about your connection to Source Energy. Start by setting the intention that you and your journey are *in the light, of the light and for the light.* For the time being, you need to call in the support of your angels, guides, and ancestors, while at the same time specifying that only the highest vibration beings are welcome in your realm, and that you are effectively shielded from anyone who lacks good intentions. You can also specify but not limit that to the Pruner, the Clippers and any other negative beings. Positively inviting in all beings who are for the highest light and highest good of the Collective.

"Next, after you have set the intention for yourself, you need to extend that intention out to the whole Community. Then, you need to immediately release the idea as if it were so."

"Why's that?" asks Maya.

"Well, just like the law of attraction doesn't understand the word no, it doesn't understand when you continue to place energy toward a fear. It sees energy toward someone or something as the request to bring you more of that thing," explains Michael. "If you sit worrying about the Clippers finding you, you are essentially attracting the Clippers to you more quickly."

"Wait a minute … let me make a comparison here for understanding. So, if I say I don't want to be lonely, I'm going to continue to be lonely because the universe didn't understand what I meant?" questions Maya.

"Hah," laughs Michael, "It's not really that the universe didn't understand, but that you did not use your words intentionally."

"Okay, let me dive a little deeper on that," clarifies Maya. "So, if I say something like, 'I want a great friend,' and I have been saying it for a while … I just need to release it?"

"Whoo!" Michael whistles. "That there is a double doozy. Based on what you said previously, one of two things could be happening … or both! Your first comment was that you are lonely, but your second is that you want a friend. So, while you may want a friend, you are placing greater emphasis on the fact that you are lonely … so you attract lonelier. Second, you said you want a great friend … and that might be exactly what you are experiencing … wanting. The universe has actually given you exactly what you asked for. Using a word like 'want' can be tricky because you are experiencing wanting. The only way to shift the tone of that word is to amplify your desire with pure emotions. Positive powerful emotions are at the root of all manifested intentions."

"Wow! Mind blown!" Maya makes an explosion symbol with her right hand next to her temple. "So, how do I change it to the positive?"

"Well," begins Michael, "You need to say it, act it, believe it, and feel as though you already have it! So, in this scenario, you could say something like, 'I am blessed to have a great friend … or great friends,' and then you need to release it and act as though you already have great friends. Believe that you do … plan outings for yourselves and imagine what it would feel like if you were actually there.

"Let's do this little exercise that can help you to improve your interactions with the law of attraction. The first is a simple tapping exercise. Take your right hand and place it over your heart. Use your three long fingers and start to rub a circle with your fingers about an inch to two beneath your collar bone. You will likely do six rotations while at the same time saying, 'I love and accept myself with ALL my problems and limitations.'"

"Really?" scoffs Maya.

"Yes, really!" grins Michael. "Three times—with the words!"

Maya rolls her eyes. "This feels really cheesy," she giggles, and starts to recite the phrase while rubbing beneath her collar bone. "I love and accept myself with ALL my problems and limitations. I love and accept myself with ALL my problems and limitations. I love and accept myself with ALL my problems and limitations."

"Good. Now use your four fingers on your right hand to tap the outside edge of your left hand—the fleshy bit where you would karate chop," he explains, "and say, 'Even though I am lonely, I STILL love and accept myself.'"

Maya rolls her eyes again and begins to tap the side of her palm. "Three times?" she confirms. When Michael nods, she continues. "Even though I am lonely, I STILL love and accept myself. Even though I am lonely, I STILL love and accept myself. Even though I am lonely, I STILL love and accept myself."

"Good. Now you are going to tap your midline in four different places saying this phrase at least once at each place. Start with the middle of your forehead, then under the nose, under the lower lip and middle of the chest. Say, 'I let go of this problem, ALL its roots and causes, from my mind, body, and soul.'"

"Really? How is this a thing?" Maya questions disbelievingly.

"It's ancient medicine. It's like acupressure for your meridians!" Michael smiles.

"My meridians?" Maya looks confused.

"Yes!" Michael responds excitedly. "Meridians are like a network of energy in your body. They carry all that you are throughout your body."

"Okay." Maya concedes. "It's not a great reason, but it's a reason."

She shifts gears. "Forehead, under the nose, under the lower lip, and middle of the chest?" Maya questions.

"Yes," Michael confirms.

Maya begins to tap the middle of her forehead while saying, "I let go of this problem, ALL its roots and causes, from my mind, body, and soul." She moves her fingers down beneath her nose. "I let go of this problem, ALL its roots and causes, from my mind, body, and soul." Then she moves beneath her bottom lip. "I let go of this problem, ALL its roots and causes, from my mind, body and soul." Finally, she taps in the centre of her chest. "I let go of this problem, ALL its roots and causes, from my mind, body, and soul."

"Great. Now, try this." Michael starts to help Maya paint a mental picture. "Close your eyes and visualize something you would like to do with friends."

Maya closes her eyes and imagines going to a local fair with friends.

"Do you have a thought?" asks Michael.

"Yes," says Maya. "We are at a local fair."

"Okay. Now, I want you to imagine everything about that day," coaxes Michael. "What are you doing? Why is it so good? What is the emotion that you are feeling?"

"Ooh, fun!" Maya glows. "We're walking down the main drag of the fairgrounds … We're smiling and laughing. We turn off into the games square. We start to play a game … one of those shooting games where you have to shoot a ball to knock over the cups in order to win the stuffed animal. We aren't very good, but we are all trying and having fun. One of my friends gets lucky and knocks all of her cups down. The staff hands her a pink and purple stuffed dog. We laugh and walk over to the ride alley. We grab tickets to ride a roller coaster and then the Tilt-a-Whirl. We keep sliding into each other and it's hilarious. I get crushed in between two of my friends and my shoulders feel pinched but I don't care. It is so much fun. When we're finished, we head over to the canteen and buy candy floss and candy apples. We're eating them and licking our lips and fingers. The cotton candy melts in your mouth. It's like wrapping your mouth around sweet air. So delicious!" Maya grins from ear to ear. She looks radiant with excitement.

"Wow! That sounds amazing, Maya!" Michael beams. "Now, I want you to keep thinking about how awesome this feels, and I want you to lock those emotions into your core by tapping and rubbing the back of your hand between pinky and ring finger tendons."

Maya grins as she rubs the back of her hand. She takes a deep breath and lets out a great sigh of relief. She beams, content.

"Wow! That's amazing! How does it work?"

"It's cool, isn't it?" confirms Michael. "It's called Emotional Freedom Technique, and as I mentioned, it's based on the idea of acupuncture. By tapping certain points, it changes the flow of energy in your body, allowing you to release old emotions surrounding your thought patterns and allowing yourself to reprogram new ideas. There is another method that balances your meridians, but this felt like the right one for the situation. I can teach you the other technique at a later time when you need it."

"Okay. Perfect! Coming back to the mission, I will set the intention for myself and the Community and then you said I need to release it?" asks Maya.

"Yes." Michael laughs, "You do. You need to release it and believe that it will happen and then allow yourself to feel as if it is happening. Now this is the tricky part. You cannot, not for one second, go back and think on that intention. You have to believe it is so. You cannot let your thoughts of fear return to that subject anymore. Is that clear?"

"Yes," Maya starts, "But Michael, what happens if I do?"

"The mission could be ruined and the Pruner will be able to sense both who you are and what message you are trying to communicate." Michael warns.

"Whoo!" It is Maya's turn to whistle. "No pressure."

"I know, right?" Michael shrugs. "Oh, one last thing. I think it would be a good idea to carry a piece of black tourmaline or black jade. Is there a gem shop in your town?"

"Yes, there is! I love that place! What are the features of those gems, other than the obvious black?" asks Maya.

"Black tourmaline is grounding and black jade is like a personal energy guardian," notes Michael. "Clear quartz might be good too as a shield or to magnify the positive energy already around you. Definitely look into those three."

"Sounds good. Can I take a break and head there now?" asks Maya.

"That's a great idea. Take a break, have a snack, and head down to the gem shop. We can start again when you get back."

THE NEXT LEVEL

"HEY MICHAEL, THAT shop is so cool!" Maya says excitedly. "There must have been thousands of little gems and jewelry, singing bowls, and knickknacks. I love it! I was able to get a clear quartz and a piece of black tourmaline. There wasn't any black jade."

"Amazing! Keep those in your pocket; they'll help you feel safe. Any time you start to feel scared, or you want to amp up your energy, you can reach into your pocket and rub them or take them out and hold them in one of your hands." explains Michael. "But Maya, know this … you do not need them. You are enough—all on your own. I offered the idea of a stone as a tool in your toolkit, but you do not need to use it as a crutch. You are a divine creator all on your own. You just need to be clear with your intentions."

"Perfect!" Maya says, as she slides them into her pocket.

"Okay, let's get back to it. Now that you know how to travel, disconnect, and set up blocks, those will help keep you safe while you are practising." Michael says. "Over the next few days, you will need to practise moving quickly and stealthily between destinations. You will also need to keep your thoughts as clear as possible before you move to ensure the Clippers aren't following your thoughts."

"How will I know if they are following me?" inquires Maya.

"You will know. It's a feeling of doom that you can't overcome." Michael sounds crushed. "If you ever feel this way, try shifting to one of your ten emergency destinations and start the Mayday message immediately."

"Okay, good tip." Maya nods.

"When practising, you're going to follow my lead," says Michael, "and progress to roughly following my script. You will call in protection. Call for all archangels to support this message. Call the archangel Raphael and the element of air to protect the east. Call in the archangel Michael and the element of fire to protect the south. Call in the archangel Gabriel and the element of water to protect the west, and call in the archangel Uriel and the element of earth to protect the north. Call in your personal team of any other archangels, ancestors, descendants and all fellow lightworkers … any questions?"

"Yes! Of course!" Maya grins. "Why do you need to specify what each archangel is bringing to the table? Aren't they all-powerful? Shouldn't they already know their role?"

"Absolutely!" Michael agrees. "But again, intention is everything, and, in this instance, we want to be very clear about what we want to see in our co-creation."

"Co-creation?" Maya questions.

Michael grins. "Yes. When we create with the law of attraction, we need to take into account that each being has their own free will and the ability to create as well. Every interaction you have with someone is an opportunity to create an experience together."

"That sounds intense and confusing." Maya notes.

"It can be," Michael agrees. "For now, just trust me. You do not always need to request specifics of angels, light-workers and such, but this is such an important message that when you make the Mayday call, I want us to put our best foot forward."

"That makes sense," agrees Maya.

"Next, you will set up blocks for yourself," Michael continues. "You won't set the intention to block the community until it's actually GO time.

"After you set up your personal block, begin to focus on your heart centre. Allow it to radiate and fill your whole bubble, and then send your light down through your chakras and connect to the earth's core. Bring that light back up through all of your chakras and out through you crown chakra, connecting in a beam of light to your heart chakra. Continue this process while calling in more and more light. Say to yourself, 'I am Light, Creator bring me light. Creator I am Light, give me light.'

"When it is GO time, this is where you will set up blocks for the Community and then start the Mayday message, but until we are ready, this is where you will shift to your next location. Try to travel to two or three places per session and change up how long you visit each place. Vary where you go each time and try not to create a pattern of where you go so that you do not create a path between time-space realities. Also, be sure to check in at home and recharge before trying again."

"Most of that sounds good, but can you explain that last part, the idea of a path between time-space reality?" Maya asks.

"Oh, yes! That is a fantastic question, Maya," Michael says. "There is a great quote by Henry David Thoreau. He said,

> A single footstep will not make a path on the earth, so a single thought will not make a pathway in the mind. To make a deep physical path, we walk again and again. To make a deep mental path, we must think over and over the kind of thoughts we wish to dominate our lives.

Just as there becomes a physical path in a forest, there is also a visible path in between time-space realities when frequently travelled pathways are used. They are subtle, but to a trained tracker, they are evident. If you were to shift from Walt Disney World to the Olympics every time, or many times when practising, there will be a sort of light residue between the two locations hidden within the molecules between time-space realities. It would tell a tracker, and in turn, the Pruner, to station the Clippers near that residue in the hopes of catching someone."

"Whoa!" exclaims Maya. "That's some high-level quantum speak!"

"Yeah, well, that's just how we roll around here!" Michael smirks. "Anyway, on GO day, as you radiate light, you will start a Mayday call to all available souls. You will beckon all available lightworkers to connect immediately. You will describe my situation quickly and briefly, adding key points about the Clippers and the Pruner. You will outline the importance of the next steps. The immediacy is important. Life as we know it has the potential to be drastically altered within the next few moments or months … With me so far?"

"Yes … it's a lot, but I'm with you." Maya replies.

"Okay. Your exact words should be something to this extent, but don't get lost in memorizing; allow yourself to flow and hold the feeling of the content deep in your heart. 'Mayday, Mayday, Mayday. Time is short. We are in grave danger. The Pruner is sending Clippers to steal your internal clocks and take away your ability to connect. We must STOP them immediately. All available lightworkers are to generate shields of light. Protect yourselves and set up blocks for yourselves and the Community as often as needed. Call in all archangels, light consciousness, and ancestors of highest vibration. Travel fast and light. Collaborate and send healing energy to all those light beings affected and to the Pruner. He was one of ours. Turned. We need solutions to solve or transmute this problem. Who has ideas?' … How does that sound?" Michael asks.

"Good." Maya takes a deep breath and sighs. "What does transmute mean?"

Michael grins. "Transmute is the idea of changing something negative into a positive by filling it with divine healing light."

"That's it?" wonders Maya.

"That's it. Transmutation is often the easy part."

Michael senses Maya's uncertainty.

"It's a lot, Maya; I know. I'm asking a lot of you. But you can do this. I know you can." Michael consoles. "Sit with it and try to learn the script for a bit. Then spend some time meditating and connecting to Source Energy via your chakras, grounding with the earth and channeling your higher self. Feel connected. Feel refreshed. Then take the night off. Don't try to travel tonight. Spend time with your mom and take a hot bath. Early to bed. You can begin practising in the morning. And Maya …"

"Yes?" she looks up, exhausted.

"Be careful not to think of anything too deep right now. I know it can be all-consuming, but do not contain thoughts beyond connection and calm. It is still too dangerous. Tap through your emotions if you need to and release any fears. Remember, when in doubt breathe … and sigh. Everyone focuses on the breath but the sigh is equally important for your body to release negative energy … and also, Maya …"

"Yes?" Maya looks up, barely able to keep her eyes open.

"I'm so proud of you. Of everything you have accomplished in a short period of time. You're doing great!" Michael praises.

"Thank you, Michael." Maya is clearly still processing. "I'm still trying to get my head around everything … so, I won't be doing the whole script and meditation altogether—at all before GO day?"

"No. It's too dangerous," warns Michael. "We need to play it safe and only launch the full energy once. You only want to call on the Collective once—it opens too many portholes and becomes too dangerous for everyone involved otherwise."

"Okay. Thanks for explaining." Maya yawns.

"Maya—you are amazing. You're doing great! You are your namesake. You can do this!"

"What does that mean?" Maya inquires. "My namesake?"

"You'll see …" Michael sidesteps the topic. "For now, go rest. You can refocus on learning the script and connecting later tonight after you've had some time to relax. Then, tomorrow after school, you can start the real preparation."

INCUBATION

MAYA SLOWLY WALKS through the backdoor to the mudroom. Her mom is working in the kitchen, baking cookies, and she glides into the mudroom, enveloping Maya into her arms.

"My love," she says, "you look exhausted. What have you been doing all this time?"

Maya grins. "Just hanging out with my friends, Mom. We had fun ... I just didn't sleep well last night." Maya fibs.

"Maybe you should go to bed early." suggests Mom.

"I should, but I'd really like to hang out with you for a bit ... and then take a hot bath." Maya muses.

"Sure thing, love." Mom grabs Maya's shoulders and looks deep into her eyes. "Is everything okay?"

"Yeah, of course." Maya shrugs, thinking about carrying the weight of the world ... and knowing she will have to do it without thinking of her mother's support or deep embrace. 'I can do this.' she thinks. 'I am my namesake.' Maya furrows her brow as she walks into the kitchen. 'What does that mean?' She turns to her mom, "Hey Mom, can we play a board game?"

"Definitely." her mom smiles. "I'm going to kick your butt!"

"You don't even know what we're playing yet!" Maya counters.

"Don't care … I am the master." Mom cackles as she walks into the living room to look at the games shelf. Maya slides in beside her and tucks under her arm for a cuddle.

"This one." Maya points toward a box. "I like figuring out which shapes fit."

"Sounds good." Mom says, and gives her a squeeze before reaching forward to grab the box.

They sit down at the dining room table and start to take the game and pieces out of the box, separating the coloured tiles into four groups. Maya's mom is supportive and grounded. She believes in her, but would she would likely think that shifting is unrealistic.

"Hey Mom," Maya asks, "what is my namesake?"

"Ooh, it's a good one!" Mom winks as she lays her first tile in the corner. "It's a Sanskrit name that has a double meaning. On one hand, it means illusion. That which we see is false. But on the other hand, it means divine creative energy, which means you can create your reality. Create your illusion, so to speak. Create the world you live in. It is based on the idea of the law of attraction. Wherever you put your thoughts and your energy is what you will see in your life. Very powerful stuff! I can't believe I haven't told you that before. I'm sure I have … you must have forgotten."

"Maybe. Perhaps it's divine timing today!" Maya smiles tiredly.

"Do tell …" Mom pushes.

"It's nothing, Mom." Maya responds. "It's just funny that someone else mentioned it today." Maya grins and places one of her pieces on the board. They continue to play and chatter happily. When they finish, Maya says that she will go take a hot bath.

As she runs the bath, she drops some lavender essential oil into the tub to help her relax and connect. She lowers herself into the tub and thinks about her day. What a weekend. She has learned so much. Maya closes her eyes and rests her head back on the bath pillow to allow her mind time to incubate all of this information. In her mind, she was psychologically arming herself with all of the tools and strength she thought she would need to be successful on her journey. She debates meditating in the tub and feels strange about it. What if all those ancestors she calls in could see her naked? She wonders what happens if she shifts to a new location while naked. Would she end up in the new location naked? Better to wait and ask Michael tomorrow.

When she finishes her bath, Maya heads down to hug her mom.

"'Night mom, I love you." Maya hugs her mom from behind, overtop of her shoulders. She stays a little longer, squeezing a little tighter.

"Good night, my love." Mom places her hands on top of Maya's hands and squeezes.

"I'm going straight to bed Mom, please don't come in and wake me?" Maya asks.

"No problem, love. Sweet dreams!" Mom says, and turns back to her book.

Maya walks upstairs to her bedroom, planning on shifting to a few of her researched locations tonight. She remembers Michael telling her to rest tonight, but she feels refreshed and rejuvenated after her bath and she wants to be ready for their discussion tomorrow after school.

Maya changes into some jeans and a nondescript T-shirt instead of her pajamas. She does not want to call attention to herself based on her clothing. Maya combs her hair and props up her pillows against her headboard. She pulls back her duvet and climbs into bed, sitting cross-legged. Maya reaches over and turns off the bedside lamp so that her mom would think she's asleep and not disturb her. She checks the time on the clock beside her bed, eight fifty-three p.m. She reaches over to grab the two gemstones that she had put on her nightstand, shoving them into her pocket to remind her to stay calm and positive.

Maya closes her eyes and grounds herself. She begins the ritual that Michael has taught her, by calling in her ancestors, guides, and beings of highest light. Maya decides she will start her practice by travelling to Walt Disney World and then the Eiffel Tower in Paris. She focuses first on Walt Disney World. Within an instant, Maya arrives in front of the Epcot stage. She stands in wonder and awe. The magnitude of all of the dancers with the awe-inspiring release of balloons—it is truly beautiful. She wants to stay and see the rest of the show, but Maya knows she is on a timeline and she needs to shift quickly and get home as fast as she can.

Within a matter of seconds, Maya shifts to Paris. She gazes up at the massive structure that towers over her. The iron structure shoots up into the sky. Looking south, she can see the sun shifting into the western sky. She memorizes this moment, knowing she will be back one day. Some day when she would be able to climb the tower and embrace the famous view out over the city.

Maya shifts home and grounds herself back into her surroundings. She takes a deep breath and lets out a deep sigh. Maya begins to wiggle her fingers and toes, rotates her neck from side to side, and opens her eyes while stretching her arms up over head. She looks around her room in the dark, checking the clock and smiles. Success!

For Maya's second trip, she decides to try two new places and one that she had already visited—the Olympics in Mexico, Walt Disney World, and the Sensō-ji Temple in Japan. Once Maya commits to grounding herself again, it happens faster and clearer than the first time. She is able to shift quickly to Mexico. It is a beautiful day. Maya gazes up the stairs to where Queta Basilio is lighting the torch to open the 1968 Olympic Games. It is a magical, history-making moment.

Maya closes her eyes, grounds, and shifts back to Walt Disney World. The second viewing is just as powerful as the first. The energy that the performers put into the show is spectacular. Regrettably, Maya knows she needs to shift again, this time heading to Japan. She lands just inside the gate, in the middle of a light rain. She looks to the little shop on her right and walks over to quickly peruse the goods that are being sold—knickknacks and such. There are little ceramic figurines of the Buddha, the temple itself, and Omamori blessings and luck charms.

She thinks about getting a lucky charm and wonders if she can even travel with something like that … and could it even help in a grave situation such as hers. Maya makes a mental note to ask Michael about it tomorrow when they check in.

She surveys the wares one more time, turns, and begins to walk away. As she walks, she closes her eyes for a split second and just like that, she is home, literally within seconds. 'How cool is this.' Maya thinks. 'I am so blessed to have this knowledge.' Maya decides to shift once more tonight and then to spend some time solidifying the difficult message that she would need to share very soon.

She decides that this next shift needs to be four places to ensure she had visited everywhere on her top ten list before meeting up with Michael tomorrow. So far, she has visited Walt Disney World, Paris, Mexico, and Japan. If she visits three more new places tonight, with one repeat, she could visit the last three in the morning before meeting up. Maya looks at her top ten list. She decides to travel to the space shuttle launch, the Calgary Stampede, and the Sydney Opera House.

Maya stands up and quietly stretches. She stands tall in mountain pose and takes a deep breath. She inhales her arms overhead and bows down into a forward fold, letting herself hang and stretch out her back. Maya inhales to a flat back and exhales back into a forward fold—something she has seen her mom do a thousand times. She grabs hold of each of her elbows and lets the weight of her arms lengthen out her back a little more. Maya moves her neck back and forth, then inhales her arms overhead and back into mountain pose. She takes a deep breath and exhales with another sigh. She completes two more rounds of the same sequence and then turns back toward her bed.

Once Maya is comfortably seated again, she reviews the four locations she is going to visit, including their order and specific details. First, she will go to the NASA space shuttle launch on July eighth, 2011, at eleven twenty-nine a.m. Then she will shift to the Sydney Opera House on October twentieth, 1973, at four fifty-three p.m., followed by the Sensō-ji Temple on June sixth, 1912, at eight-fifteen a.m. Finally, Maya will go to the Calgary Stampede on July tenth, 1950, at six-thirty p.m.

Maya closes her eyes and prepares herself to shift. When she arrives at the space shuttle launch, she is blown away by the intensity of the noise. Even though the crowd is miles away behind the fences, the sound of the blowers is deafening. She glances around briefly, looking to the clock and creating a few memories in her mind, then leaves as quickly as she arrived.

Maya arrives beneath the flagpole at the base of the steps of the Sydney Opera House. She stumbles over and sits down on the steps. Maya puts her head down and covers her ears. She takes a few deep breaths. 'Earplugs.' she thinks. 'I need to ask Michael if I can take earplugs with me. That was seriously loud!' Maya takes a deep breath and looks up at the Opera House. It really is a magnificent creation. Maya watches the flags blow in the wind. She embraces the warmth and the sunshine as she observes the crowds walking up the stairs to enter the Opera House.

Maya takes another deep breath and sinks into grounding. Her goal this time, when visiting Japan, is to touch down and leave within five seconds. She arrives, looks to the shop on the right and shifts right over to the Calgary Stampede. 'Wow!' Maya thinks, 'I can't believe I was in Japan for a flash of a second … it barely feels like it happened.' Maya begins looking around at this new place. While she has seen elements of the stampede online, she had no idea it would feel like this. She is enthralled with the energy. Maya has been to small horse events, but never *the* stampede before. It appears to have multiple events going on simultaneously in different areas. Maya can hear a country singer in the background. The man in front of her is riding a wild horse that is bucking like crazy, and he is trying to stay on. It is equally fascinating and terrifying at the same time. Maya cannot look away. She watches until the man falls off. He hobbles away as the horse continues to buck its way to the other side of the arena. Maya makes a mental note to come back and explore the stampede further.

She shifts home and takes a huge breath. What a night. It's hard to believe she has travelled to seven different places in under a minute—according to her clock.

Maya quietly gets up and changes into her pajamas, mulling over everywhere she has visited. It's truly unfathomable. She can't wait to try this when there isn't an imminent danger. 'I wonder if I can teach Mom and take her with me.' Maya thinks. 'Yet another thing to ask Michael.'

Maya climbs back into bed and tucks herself in. She begins to think about the Mayday message. 'Once I

ground and connect, I will set up the archangels, ancestors, and collective consciousness to protect this commu-
nication. Next, I will set up the block intention excluding
the Pruner, the Clippers, and any negative allies, allowing only beings of the highest and purest intention. Next
is saying Mayday three times, calling in all available
lightworkers and then immediately transmitting, 'Time
is short. We are in grave danger. The Pruner is sending
Clippers to steal your internal clocks and take away your
ability to connect. We must STOP them immediately.
All available lightworkers are to generate shields of light.
Protect yourselves and set up blocks for yourself and the
Community as often as needed. Call in all archangels,
light consciousness, and ancestors of highest vibration.
Travel fast and light. Collaborate and send healing energy
to all those light beings affected and to the Pruner. He was
one of ours. Turned. We need solutions to solve or transmute this problem. Who has ideas?'"

Maya lets out a deep sigh. It feels good, but she practices one more time. After she runs through the script
once more, she smiles to herself contentedly. 'I can do
this. I've got this!' She snuggles down into her blankets
and drifts off to sleep almost immediately.

As the sun beams in from outside the window, Maya stirs
slightly. A smile spreads across her face. She feels rested
after a crazy weekend of taking in so much information.
Maya stretches her body long, reaching her toes out of her
blankets and pushing her hands against the wall behind

her. She yawns into the stretch and opens her eyes. It is later than she had hoped, but she is grateful to feel rested. She still has time to shift quickly before her mom comes in to wake her.

In looking over her top ten list, Maya decides she will visit the peaceful COVID protest in London first, and then the Great Wall of China. Next, she will shift back to the Calgary Stampede, and then end on the beaches of Palolem in Goa.

Maya quietly gets dressed in the same nondescript jeans and T-shirt. She grabs a mask and puts it on her wrist. Maya props up her pillows again and sits down to prepare herself for one last journey this morning before enduring what will no doubt feel like an excruciatingly long day at school before meeting up with Michael. She goes through her start-up routine of grounding, connecting, and blocking, then she sets the intention to arrive in London, England, in front of Buckingham Palace on April twentieth, 2020, at twelve-twenty p.m. Within a moment she is there, standing amongst the hustle and bustle of the crowds. She quickly pulls her mask on and looks around for key markers. Maya looks to her left at the guard with his tall hat and stoic demeanor. She peers through the gates, into the palace. Then she goes inward again.

'The view is spectacular,' Maya gasps, standing at the topmost building in Jinshanling. Many tourists are stopping here to take pictures of the extravagant scenery. Maya leans against the building to allow more people to get between her and the photographers. It is very busy. It may be a difficult place to transmit the Mayday message.

She takes in the breathtaking view one more time, then shifts back to the Calgary Stampede.

The second time around it is still just as wonderful. The cowboys are so animated, and clearly love their lifestyle. Maya smiles and spins around, taking it in, and then shifts almost immediately to Palolem Beach.

Shifting is becoming easier; she needs less time to ground and connect. It feels as if her cells remember what she is supposed to do.

South Goa is gorgeous. Maya collapses onto the sand and soaks up the heat, feeling the sand squeeze between her fingers and toes. She lies down and stretches on the beach, looking up and seeing the yellow wooden sign on the Dreams of Palolem beach hut.

'This is the life.' Maya thinks. 'Sun, sand, and water as far as the eye can see.' While it isn't the most majestic of places, it is by far her favourite. She will definitely need to come back here to swim and check out the local activities in the future.

And just like that, Maya is back in her bedroom. She takes a deep breath in and lets out a sigh of relief … or a sigh of amazement. She wiggles her fingers and toes, rolls her neck and opens her eyes. Maya rubs her eyes as she yawns. 'It's amazing that I can feel so tired a few minutes after waking up and yet also equally energized by such amazing experiences.' Maya thinks.

Looking at her bedside clock, Maya realizes she needs to get moving. She rushes into the bathroom to shower and brush her teeth.

CHECK-IN

AFTER BREAKFAST, MAYA packs her bag for school and throws in a few extra snacks, a blanket, and a book. She kisses her mom goodbye. As expected, the school day feels like it is never going to end. Even her favourite classes feel like the teacher is droning on. When the final bell rings, Maya is so excited she is practically buzzing in her chair. She runs out of the building so fast; she nearly takes out a classmate on her way through the door.

Once she arrives at the park, she sets up her blanket and her book and looks around at what is happening at the park today. She makes a mental note of the date and time.

"Good afternoon, Michael." Maya starts.

"Hi, Maya! How was your day?" Michael responds.

"Long!" Maya says in exasperation.

"I hear you," Michael agrees. "And how was last night?"

"It was so amazing! I relaxed with my mom for a bit, took a hot bath, and got so excited to travel that I checked out my top ten. I am shocked at how quickly I was able to shift at the end." Maya notes.

"Oh, wow! That's great Maya! I can't believe you were so productive after such a long day!" Michael pumps her up. "It is so cool when you start to shift quickly; just be careful to always check in to make sure you are in the correct time-space reality. How did it feel when you were shifting quickly?"

"It was good. It felt sort of unreal. I can't believe I was even there—I was able to shift once in under five seconds … I do have a lot of questions though," mentions Maya.

"Ask away," Michael allows.

"Well, for starters," Maya begins, "I asked my mom about my namesake last night and she explained that it has a double meaning."

"Yes," replies Michael, "that's true. What else did she say?"

"She said that on one hand, Maya in Sanskrit means illusion, but on the other hand, it means divine creative energy."

"Yes! Exactly!" Michael replies emphatically.

Maya looks puzzled. "What exactly does that mean?"

"Ah," Michael beams. "It means that what we see, or what we think we know about our lives is all an illusion. It is all sort of—fake, like watching a TV show. We, as humans, have great power to create our experiences. It's been said many times, but humans have a really hard time understanding the concept. The law of attraction has been passed down to knowledge keepers for centuries. There are a few compounding ideas, but in essence, the law of attraction means, in general—if you truly believe you can create your external life—you will! You will find a way to clear any limited beliefs you have and set clear, consistent messaging to yourself every day. Your name attributes you with having great power at wielding or manipulating your reality."

"Wow! I do remember being told that," Maya responds. "But I have never quite understood how to create or how to believe it is possible. It's a little airy fairy, isn't it?"

"Airy fairy or not, it's the truth! It's a universal law so it must be true!" responds Michael.

"Then why are so many people unhappy? Why aren't they getting what they want?" asks Maya.

"Well, we actually talked about this earlier, Maya. The same scenario applies here and in most situations. Most times, we may say we want something, but our beliefs about it and our feelings around it are much different in the grand scheme of things and so we experience wanting rather than receiving. In other ways, we might say we want something, but we are blocking it coming to fruition because we secretly tell ourselves it is not possible."

"Oh, right!" says Maya. "We did talk about this. I totally remember. So how does that affect my namesake?"

"Ideally, you will learn quickly how much you can actually affect your surroundings, and with impeccable words and focused emotions, you will be able to quickly create!" Michael says.

"Quickly create? … Anything?" queries Maya.

"Anything that you put your mind, beliefs, actions, and emotions into!" answers Michael.

"Amazing!" shouts Maya, "What can I do to start that now?"

"Well, there are lots of simple tricks to make changes. There are so many that I think it is best to focus on these lessons after we save the world, but I will tell you this ... each time you catch yourself 'wanting' something, shift your statement to 'I am, I have, or I am enjoying; I am grateful for, I receive or I choose ...' and then visualize what it would feel like to actually have that 'wish' already. Then release the want and continue to imagine that you already have it. The other quick trick I can tell you before we move on, is every time you catch yourself saying something negative, reframe the situation to something positive with three new phrases, and feel the positivity in those phrases."

"Can you please give me an example?" asks Maya.

"Yes, of course," says Michael. "I'm walking down the street and I notice that there is graffiti on the wall. I might catch myself saying, 'That is some ugly graffiti, why would anyone deface property like that?' I immediately switch to a more positive outlook. 'Wow! Look at that graffiti, that is amazing artistry. It is wonderful that artists are finding new outlets and locations to showcase their work. I wonder if graffiti artists are able to learn from each other's artwork?' Does that make sense?"

"Yes! Absolutely!" smiles Maya. "Thank you for sharing!"

"Do you want to try one?" asks Michael.

"Ooh, good idea," Maya nods. "Okay. I'm walking down the street and I notice that a woman is wearing a very unflattering sweater. I immediately think of three things that I like in this situation. She has beautiful eyes and a kind smile, plus, her shoes are super stylish.'"

"Great job, Maya!" One more thing, Michael notes. "You have to be careful with judgment. Judging others is the fastest way we keep ourselves trapped in a loop of discontent. The universe does not understand that we are speaking about other people or things. It then gives us more discontent and judgment. It is very important to get out of the habit of judging."

"Oh, okay. I didn't mean anything by it," Maya apologizes.

"No worries, we all do it—It's just very important to curb the habit before it becomes out of control." responds Michael.

Maya nods in agreement. "And how do you do that?"

"By doing exactly what we just talked about—state three positive things each time you catch yourself saying something negative. Eventually, positivity will take over and become your dominant response. Isn't that amazing?" Michael checks in.

"That is amazing!" Maya smiles. "Okay, next question. It's a bit embarrassing, but very important! What happens if I meditate or shift naked … or if I need something in a new place, like different clothing or a mask?"

"Oh, amazing question!" laughs Michael. "Yes, meditating naked is fine—no one outside of us cares about the bodily form. Shifting naked on the other hand, can be embarrassing if you don't catch yourself mid-travel. As you ground yourself, imagine that you are already wearing clothing. This also works for things like masks or backpacks, but this is where doing your research helps as well. It's as if you are doing a wardrobe change in a play.

You can imagine you're wearing clothing suited to the time and location, and you will arrive at your next location already dressed to fit in. However, if you don't have that research, there is another trick you can do, that we are going to talk about in a bit."

"Oh, that's fantastic," agrees Maya. "I was wearing the same nondescript jeans and a T-shirt to ensure I didn't look out of place anywhere, but I did feel a bit out of place in Japan, where clearly jeans were not yet very popular, nor red hair for that matter!"

"Yeah, right, you do call a lot of attention to yourself with your hair," giggles Michael. "You have a couple options … Wearing your hair in a low bun or braid might be a good start, and then you can change up your hat based on location and time period. It is also possible to shift your physical appearance, but honestly that takes a lot of practice and honing of your skills, and frankly, we just don't have that kind of time right now. Stick with a hat for now and we can play with that skill later."

"Okay, perfect," answers Maya. "My last two questions are more about the future, but the one might pertain. First, will I eventually be able to teach my mom how to shift and travel with her? And second, can I bring things back from these places? For instance, there was a good luck token in Japan that I had wanted, but I wasn't sure if objects would travel, or if it could disrupt the time-space reality continuum."

"Ooh, also good questions. Yes, you will be able to teach your mom, once all of this is said and done—if we are the victors—I mean when we are the victors!"

Michael catches himself in doubt. "Technically, you can bring things from the place you travel, but it *can* cause problems. For instance, if someone sees them and can't put together why you would have something from Japan, or if you make a mistake and say you visited there and yet you don't actually have proof that you travelled. It can become riddled with questions and strange accusations. For now, it is better to leave each place clean. Sort of like no-trace camping or hiking. Take nothing, leave nothing, cover your tracks. Does that make sense?"

Once Maya nods, Michael adds, "So if that is that last of your questions—how were the locations you shifted to?"

"Really great! I can't wait to go back some day and explore each location. Are you going to meet me somewhere today?" asks Maya.

"I'll certainly try!" grins Michael.

CO-PLANNING

MICHAEL AND MAYA look at her travel plans in more detail. He asks her to review the order in which she shifted to each place.

"Okay," Maya lays it out, "First, I went to Walt Disney World and Paris. Next, I went to Mexico, revisited Walt Disney World, and then checked out the Sensō-ji Temple in Japan. Third, I visited NASA, the Sydney Opera House, revisited Japan, and then I went to the Calgary Stampede. Then, this morning, I went to a peaceful Covid protest in London, the Great Wall of China, back to Calgary, and then I ended on the beaches of Palolem in South Goa."

"What a great place to end! Good choice!" agrees Michael. "Okay. I want to try meeting you in a different capacity. I am a little unsure of a couple things. For starters, I want us to pick three places to shift to that are on your top ten list, but in a different order than you have already travelled to. Where would you like to go first?"

"Let's start in Goa, then shift to the Great Wall of China, and lastly visit NASA. I'm warning you; NASA is loud so I want to get in and out," Maya explains.

"Sounds good," Michael agrees. "However, I want you to change up the order, but don't tell me! I know you are doing these three places and I know when you will be there. I am going to try to meet up with you there without knowing when you are going. Oh, one more thing … I need you to actually ask someone or find out the time while you are there to ensure it is the time you planned to visit. Does that make sense?" he asks, and after Maya nods, he adds, "Don't forget, confirm the time!"

"Got it," Maya confirms. "Get the time in each location. Will you be there with me to confirm the time?"

"I might be." Michael wavers, "I'm not sure yet. We will see! If I'm not there, check these three locations and confirm the time and then come straight back here to discuss."

"Sounds good. Anything else?" Maya checks.

"Yes! Use this second wave of shifts as an opportunity to practice a bit more. Think back to what outfits you saw people wearing when you visited last night or this morning. Try to change into those outfits before you arrive."

Michael pauses and starts laughing. Maya giggles and eventually asks, "What's up? What's so funny?"

"Oh, my goodness." Michael laughs, "I am so sorry. I was remembering the first time I really understood this lesson. I was young … maybe seven or eight. I can't remember where I was shifting to, but mid-shift, I thought of a clown at a circus … and poof, I arrived as a clown."

Maya laughed out loud.

"That image alone is hilarious, but it doesn't stop there," Michael continues. "Clowns, in the modern sense, had not yet been invented past the local jester stage and it was incredibly awkward to explain the multicoloured plastic wig that almost had me burned at the stake for being some kind of weird male witch. Luckily, I was able to snap out of it and find a new thought to shift to ... but shifting while being watched by non-shifters is very difficult. Their fears are present in daily life even though they do not believe in any sort of time travel. The best advice I can give you is that if you mistakenly arrive somewhere unprepared—shift immediately to a new location and you can go back to that location at a later time with more preparation."

"That is hilarious! Thanks for the tip," Maya says graciously. "How does shifting normally not bother people?"

"Well, normally, if you see someone quickly and then they are gone, you chalk it up to your imagination ... but when you are actually watching someone, and they disappear, it is much more difficult to explain to yourself." Michael explains.

"So what happens on those rare occasions when someone has to shift in front of people?" wonders Maya.

"Well, many people may still think it must have been their imagination, or that their eyes have played a trick on them," Michael pauses, "But others experience an elemental shift that sends out a frequency to the universe that they are ready for mentorship—to learn the mysteries hidden beneath our sight. Mentors are alerted to keep an eye on these people and to impart pertinent knowledge as they seem ready."

"Huh, that makes sense." Maya responds.

"Are you ready to go? Michael asks.

"Yes!" Maya closes her eyes and starts her grounding routine. When she arrives at NASA, she is proud of herself for wearing protective headphones. The visit is so much more enjoyable this way. She spins around quickly, looking for Michael, and looks at the big countdown clock. She knows it is the right time, but she asks a bystander the time anyway, just to confirm—eleven twenty-nine a.m.

Maya shifts to Goa, mid-shift she pictures wearing a bright peach bikini and holding a drink with an umbrella in her hand, and immediately feels the relief of standing in the sand. She takes a sip of her fruity drink and sets it down in the sand. She quickly runs and dives into the waves. 'One extra minute can't hurt,' she thinks. As she's walking out of the water she calls out to Michael. Nothing. Maya walks up to a couple bathing in the sun and asks for the time. Bang on … two for two. One more attempt.

As Maya shifts to the Great Wall of China, she thinks of the tourists. She arrives with a braid, an olive-coloured button-down shirt tied at the waist over a blue sports bra, khaki shorts, and hiking shoes with fantastically comfortable socks. These wardrobe changes are the best! She briefly looks for Michael and calls out his name again. Nothing—again, Maya turns to a tourist who she hears speaking English and asks time. Three for three. She shifts back home, still in the hiking gear.

"Michael?" she asks, as soon as she grounds.

"Hi! It didn't work. I'm sorry." Michael says sheepishly.

"That's okay! Why do you think that happened? You were able to go to my birthday," Maya questions.

"I am not completely sure, but I am guessing I was able to go to the birthday party because I knew that you would be there exactly when I tried to contact you. In today's scenario, I was guessing. I'm clearly attached to you in some capacity, and not knowing the specifics roots me to this time-space reality where we are guaranteed a connection. In the grand scheme of things, it's not that big a deal, but it would have been cool if I could have joined you."

"Is there any other way?" asks Maya.

Michael explains, "If the only way that I can shift is to be attached to you and know where you are going in advance, it is far too dangerous and it is not worth risking the mission. If the Clippers are able to figure out that you are shifting—or that you have the power to bring me with you—it would only be a matter of time before you became their top priority to find. Once the Clippers figure out that you're a shifter, your home base will be compromised until the final Community gathering."

Michael pauses, letting the gravity of the situation sink in. "Think about it Maya," he urges. "Every moment now with your family and friends is potentially the last … or the last for a very long time. Take this time to love them, acknowledge them, and to speak wisely in their presence. Be careful not to give anything away, but truly appreciate each moment."

"Alright. Thank you." Maya sits quietly thinking, breathing deeply. A smile creeps across her face as she thinks of her mom.

Michael gives her a few more minutes to ponder her family and then asks, "So, how did it go today?"

"Oh, right!" Maya reconnects to Michael. "It was so cool! I arrived at NASA with protective earphones on and then I consciously called in a bikini and a drink on the beach, and then just thinking about the hikers on the wall, I arrived in hiking gear. It was the best high-speed fashion show ever! I'm actually still in hiking clothes now ... why didn't I switch back?"

"Oh! Interesting! You are progressing so fast! I am really proud of you. I will caution you on one more thing today. You returned to your time in different clothing. Today it isn't too bad because you might wear hiking clothes to the park, but what if it had been a bikini?" Michael asks rhetorically and continues speaking. "Plus, while no one at the park will mind, I bet your mom would be pretty interested in finding out where you got the new digs."

"What should I do to fix it?" asks Maya.

"Well, you're not done yet for the day so you can change during the next shift ... or if you don't think too many people are watching you, you can change now. You will likely be safer in this moment to just wait until you shift again. In a pinch, if you need to shift in front of people, do it as fast as possible and if they look at you funny, act as if they have seen a ghost and walk away in character."

"Okay, sounds good. Where else am I going today?" asks Maya.

UPPING THE ANTE

"OUR BEST DEFENSE is that you are currently an unknown entity to the Collective and the Pruner. The better and faster you can be at shifting before we introduce you, the safer we will be," Michael starts. "There are two other strategies that you can use to help throw the Clippers off your location. The first is more intricate than the shifting you have done so far, but this is still quite a simple strategy. The second will take a bit more practice."

"Okay," answers Maya. "What's the first strategy?"

"I'd like you to practice going to more diverse places. For instance, Paris in medieval times at dusk, or the Stone Age. Try visiting places that are less common. Also, I'd like you to continue to practice changing your look while shifting."

"Okay. Cool," says Maya. "So, does that mean I now need to research all of these places?"

"Not this time. We're going to try something new," answers Michael. "You're doing amazing with shifting, and I think it will be good for you to up the ante."

"Up the ante?" questions Maya, "Like in poker?"

"Yes, sort of," laughs Michael. "Your strength in shifting has been growing; it's a good time for you to try to choose a date and time in space and shift with no knowledge of what you are getting into."

"How is that safe?" asks Maya.

"Well, it is just a different type of safety," explains Michael. "When you shift and know every detail, you are much safer. But you are also emitting a frequency of where you are heading, and truthfully, this is where the Clippers' tracking is confusing. We don't really know how they are doing it, but we do know that when we think of heading somewhere, it can be tracked; so, if you pick a new location and time in the moment, it is less likely to be picked up on.

"So, if you start to get tracked, you need to know there are other options or places that you can shift to quickly without the Clippers having advance knowledge of your typical travel plans."

"Is there anything else I need to consider?" wonders Maya.

"This is the cool part," Michael notes. "You will need to choose your date, time and place and then begin to ground. As you are grounding, just before you start to feel yourself shift—get in tune and ask the question, 'What do I need to know about entering this time-space reality?' Your intuition, higher self, and guides will fill in the rest. You will, as if by magic, appear dressed in the appropriate clothing and prepared for whatever situation awaits you on the other side. If you are appearing in a dangerous situation, you will have a weapon in your hand. Attempt to do no harm. Walk away from the situation, hide, or shift immediately.

"What happens if I can't get out before being attacked?" wonders Maya.

"Well, I didn't really want to tell you this," says Michael, "but from my experience, it is almost as if you already know everything you need to know. If you are holding a bow, you will know how to wield it. The same is true for any weapon. If needed, you will know how to do hand-to-hand combat. But honestly, nonviolence is a precept of the Collective. If at all possible, shift to a new time-space reality and completely avoid all fighting. If unavoidable, use self-defence until you can shift."

"Okay, great. That actually makes me feel better," agrees Maya. "I wasn't sure I could fight anyway!"

"If you have to, you should be able to defend yourself," confirms Michael. "You *will* have the skills you need, but the most important thing is to ground yourself as soon as possible and get yourself out of there. Danger is danger, and we do not need that fear nor fear-based energy in our fields."

"So that's the first strategy," says Maya. "What's the second?"

"The second tactic is a little more difficult." Michael pauses. "While you are shifting, you can actually think about a different location. The trick is to still shift and keep your intention and intuition focused on the first location, but you'll make anyone tracking you think you are going to the second location. It can be very hard to do … but I think it is important that you at least try it a couple times before we start."

Maya sits with a look of confusion on her face.

"Do you want to sit and think about it for a bit?" Michael offers. "It's a lot to think about."

"Yes," Maya nods. "It's a lot to take in. I think I will go for a walk around the park and have a snack."

"Great plan," Michael agrees. "Want me to come with you, or give you some time on your own?"

"I think I just need some time to think on my own, Michael," Maya frowns. She stands up, stretches, and bends down to get her banana. She opens her banana and walks toward the path that circles the outer edges of the park. She looks both ways, takes a deep breath, and decides to walk to the right.

'Intuition,' she thinks. 'Mom talks to me about that all the time. Intuition is the easy part. Think about a question … and trust the answer you hear as truth coming from your higher self. How do I feel about this situation?' *Scared.* 'Yup! What do I need to do in this situation?' *Find calm and do exactly what Michael has told you to do.* 'Okay. What do I need to do first?' *Eat your banana. Finish your walk. Then resume.* 'Resume what?' *Pick up with Michael where you just left off.* Maya takes a deep breath and exhales loudly, relaxing her shoulders. She finishes her banana and places the peel in a garbage bin that she passes on the path. She continues around the outside path, back to her blanket on the grass. She stretches her arms overhead and sits back down.

"Okay, Michael. I'm ready for the intuition task."

"Amazing. Remember, ground, get in tune, pick a date, time and place, and then as you start to shift, ask the question, 'What do I need to know about entering this time-space reality?' Got it?" Michael checks.

"I do," confirms Maya.

"Okay," Michael nods. "Good luck! I'll be here when you get back."

Maya nods, grounds herself, and synchronizes with Source Energy. She thinks to herself, 'London, England, September sixteenth, 1910, three-fifty p.m. 'What do I need to know about entering this time-space reality?' Maya asks herself. *You need to be dressed in a burgundy skirt, tight at the waist and billowing out at the bottom. White blouse, frilly around the neck. Black boots, lace-up, with a slight heel. Trimmed Edwardian, hard-brimmed hat with a dark blue-and-white striped ribbon wrapped around the band. Walk down the street and spin your parasol slowly over your shoulder. Act like you belong there.* It all happens within seconds. 'Amazing,' Maya thinks as she arrives in the exact outfit that popped into her mind. She slowly spins her parasol and walks down the street. She turns to a gentleman on the street and calmly asks him if he has the time of day.

He responds, "Three fifty-one."

Maya smiles and begins to ground. 'Stonehenge, May twenty-first, 1755, eight-fifty a.m. What do I need to know about entering this time-space reality?' *Arrive in worn clothing, as if white worn brown. Hair tied up under a flat cap. Look more like a boy. Stay on the outskirts of the rocks. Watch for people. Don't stay long. It is not always safe here.* Maya arrives on edge. She crouches down and looks around. There is no one around, but in trusting her intuition, she decides to not stay long. She takes one moment to look at the towering structures and wonder at their significance, then she quickly grounds again.

'Paris. December twenty-fifth, 1314, nine a.m. In front of Notre-Dame Cathedral,' she thinks. 'What do I need to know about entering this time-space reality?' *You're best to dress like a beggar. Have your cap in hand and wait near the bottom of the steps at the front entrance. It is nearly morning mass, so there should be lots of people there.* Maya arrives with her cap in hand, wearing tattered clothing with mud smudged on her face. 'It's sort of like the best acting school and costume change of my life!' she muses. Maya looks up at the towering cathedral. It is hard to even imagine how this was built so long ago without modernized cranes and machinery. She looks over the intricate stonework and then turns to take in the Middle Ages. 'It is really unfathomable that I am standing here right now.' Maya thinks. 'I need to better understand how this is all possible once I find Michael.'

"*Bonjour Madame, est-ce que vous avez l'heure, s'il vous plaît?*" Maya asks, and is shocked that she has greeted the woman and asked the time in French because she had been thinking of speaking in English a minute ago.

"*Oh, pauvre fille, c'est neuf heure du matin. Est-ce que je peux t'aider? J'ai des morceaux de nourriture dans ma calèche.*" The woman calls her a poor girl and tells Maya that it is nine in the morning. She asks her if she can help and notes that she has some small pieces of food in her carriage.

"*Merci beaucoup, c'est trop gentil, mais je dois partir maintenant.*" Maya says "Thank you very much, it's very kind, but I need to leave right now." Maya turns and walks away down the street. She smiles to herself, grounds, and thinks of home, remembering to shift back into the clothing she had put on in the morning.

"Hi Michael! Are you there?" Maya asks.

"Hey Maya! I'm here! Where else can I be?" Michael laughs playfully. "How did it go?"

"It went really well! I love the idea that we have all the answers within us," Maya says, "and we just have to ask!"

"It is super cool." Michael smiles. "There will be times when you don't feel connected to the answers … not when travelling, but when asking questions about your own direction. When that happens, take a break and come back to that question at a later time."

"Oh, okay." Maya looks confused. "Why does that happen?"

"There are a few reasons. It may be that on the physical plane, you are not ready for the information," Michael explains, "or it may be that the how or what you are asking is not as important as the feeling surrounding the question. It may also be that the answer is there, just on the other side of the veil, but you're not focused or in tune enough to hear it today."

"Um," Maya pauses, "that was heavy … I didn't understand all of it … what is the physical plane and a veil?"

"The physical plane," Michael starts, "is here … where you live in a physical body. There are many other planes, or levels of existence, but physicality is at the base. It's best if we leave further exploration of this until later. It is a big and confusing topic that could honestly take us months to really dive into."

"Of course," Maya grins. "And a veil?

"The veil of illusion is the difference between the known and the unknown," Michael begins. "It is the idea of pulling back the layers between the different realms or planes and revealing a greater and more widespread reality. An existence that you never even knew existed. It's like I mentioned yesterday. Right now, you are living in the physical plane, which is an illusion. The toils, the struggles, even the joy, are all a representation for you to learn or to experience. You are now in an evolution, so to speak. You are starting to see that there is more than meets the eye. The veil, the thin sheath of material or cosmic matter that has been shielding your vision, is starting to disintegrate as you learn more about the universal possibilities … Does that make sense?"

"Wow! That makes a lot of sense. Thank you for explaining," Maya says graciously while nodding and taking it all in.

"Okay, next up," Michael pushes. "It's time to face the hard stuff."

"Okay," agrees Maya. "Can you walk me through it one more time?"

"Sure," Michael grins. "For starters, remember that this is like a practice arena. You are safe to practise shifting at this stage. The only way you would need to switch roles and start broadcasting the Mayday message would be, if for some reason, the Clippers find you before we actually plan to broadcast. So, one mantra you can say to yourself before shifting, is, 'I am safe.' You always want to put out a positive intention before you shift.

"Remember, the law of attraction doesn't understand the negative, so if you are saying you are fearful, or you are saying I don't want to do something wrong … wrong and fear are what you will attract. So, always start with 'I am safe' and 'I am succeeding for my highest good,' or 'I am succeeding for the highest good of the universe,' or 'I am of service to the highest good of the universe.' That way, you have set the positive intention before you ground."

"Okay, thanks," Maya nods. "That makes me feel a bit better. I'm a little more nervous about this stage. I'm not sure why."

FILLING
THE VESSEL

"WHY DON'T YOU go for another walk, Maya," Michael suggests. "Take time to stand under the trees and take in their grounding and rooted energy. Then look up to the sky and soak up the growth energy from the sun. Imagine the sun filling up each of your chakras starting at the base and climbing to the crown.

"I want you to focus on filling your vessel. Even though we sometimes feel empty, it is literally impossible for us to be empty of life force energy. However, there are tricks we can do to fill ourselves up to maximum capacity, to feel re-energized and full of life and vitality. On your walk, connect to Source Energy and truly visualize the grounding technique I initially taught you. Visualize the ball of energy moving from your heart centre down through your hips and legs down into the earth and then back up to the sky through your crown chakra. Once you have done that, and you feel full of positive energy and ready to dive back in, we can. I don't want you to start any phase of this process with negativity or fear in your heart."

"That's a great idea. I love that you are giving me the time to process this calmly."

"Maya," Michael genuinely smiles, "you are my saviour at this point. If I rush you, I risk this whole initiative failing. While in the grand scheme of things, we are doing this for the Collective, there is still a part of me that is hoping."

"Hoping for what?" Maya scrunches her eyes and nose.

"Hoping that once you make contact with the Collective, you will also connect with my brother and other lightworkers who can help you come and find me. I am hoping that our grand charade will hold the power to somehow release me from this curse of living nowhere. Living in no time, no space, where I will surely die."

"Michael," Maya replies, a bit shocked, "it has never crossed my mind that that isn't what we are doing. I see it very clearly. Finding and rescuing you."

Michael lets out a curt giggle of relief, "Well, if you can see it, Maya, with all your infinite power, it must be true!"

"You really think I have infinite power?" Maya beams.

"The secret is, Maya, we all do!" Michael grins. "We all have the power to create our surroundings. We all just unfold to the power at different stages. You are getting a super crash course. A MasterClass!" Michael laughs at the MasterClass joke he made, a trend currently taking over the Internet by life coaches.

"Okay, what's next?" Maya asks.

"You are going to do one more chakra activity today. What you will need today is the colours, the seed sounds, and one of the mantras or affirmations that goes along with each chakra."

"That sounds like a lot of information," says Maya. "Can I please jot down some notes about the chakras and each of the qualities surrounding them? Chakras have come up a couple times now and I don't want to forget anything."

"Of course, take your time." Michael walks Maya through the exercise, pausing for her to make notes. "Once you have grounded with the trees and the sun, you can start to imagine a ball of red energy growing at the base of your spine in the first chakra, also named the root chakra. If you'd like, you can envision exhaling negative energy by spinning in a counter clockwise motion; once you feel like you have released all of the negativity from this area, begin to spin it clockwise thinking 'I am safe', 'I am secure,' or 'I am rooted.' You do not to visualize a spinning wheel, but sometimes it helps new visualizers to have something specific to focus on.

"After releasing the negative energy, as you refuel with positive mantras, visualize the candy apple red and hum the seed sound of LAM. Say it three times to start, like this: L-A-A-A-M, L-A-A-A-M, L-A-A-A-M. You will know if you need to stay with this chakra longer. You will sense if you need to keep humming. This is also a good time to ask yourself if this chakra needs a different colour to help balance itself out. Be open to whatever you sense or hear.

"If you are ready to move on, you will focus your attention on the second chakra, the sacral chakra, which is bright orange and rests in your belly.

"Again, you can visualize the chakra spinning counter clockwise to release any negative thoughts or energy, or you can just imagine yourself releasing any negative thoughts or energy connected to this chakra. Once it feels clear, start spinning the chakra clockwise while thinking, 'I am joy. I am divine creative energy,' chanting the seed sound VAM. Like this: V-A-A-A-M, V-A-A-A-M, V-A-A-A-M. Again, if this chakra is full of enough energy at this point, your body will sense that it can move on. Otherwise, you will sense that you need to keep chanting, saying this mantra, visualizing the colour orange or adding in another colour to balance the energy.

"When you're ready, move onto the third chakra, the solar plexus. Your solar plexus is located just below your sternum. Again, wring out the negative energy and begin visualizing a bright yellow like the sun. Think about the mantra 'I am graceful power' and chant RAM like this: R-A-A-A-M, R-A-A-A-M, R-A-A-A-M.

"When you're finished, move onto the fourth chakra, the heart chakra. This is a loving green energy. Exhale and spin off the negative, inhale and chant YAM while continuously thinking of the mantra, 'I am love, I forgive myself, I forgive others.' Y-A-A-A-M, Y-A-A-A-M, Y-A-A-A-M.

"Next is the fifth chakra, the throat chakra; it deals with communicating clearly. Both speaking and hearing the truth and reality. Once you clear it, think of bright blue and the mantra 'I communicate with ease. I speak and hear clearly.' The seed sound is HAM, like this: H-A-A-A-M, H-A-A-A-M, H-A-A-A-M. I sometimes find this chakra takes a few more repetitions to feel clear and full. In the beginning, we sometimes get caught up in our daily lives, in the illusions we feel that we see in front of us. Stay with it as long as you feel you should.

"Next is the sixth chakra, the third eye chakra. Visualize indigo light streaming into this spot. Unwind the negative out and then focus the indigo light filling it up as you say 'I am intuitive. I see beyond the veil.' You will chant the traditional OM, but when chanted out loud it stretches to three independent syllables, like this: A-U-M, A-U-M, A-U-M. Repeat this for as long as you need, and then focus your attention on your crown chakra.

"Clear it and then visualize white or violet light filling it up with Source Energy. You will again focus on the seed sound Om, but this time it will be repeated silently in your mind along with the mantras 'I am present. I am one: ॐ OM, ॐ OM, ॐ OM.' Stand in this bliss for as long as you need. Listen for any signs or messages from Source.

"After you have received any messages from Source, you will ground yourself back down through all of your chakras and into the earth. When you are ready, come back to me here and we can begin again."

Maya looks pensive. "It sounds amazing ... but long. Will you be okay for that long?

"Of course," Michael laughs. "I have nowhere else to be. This is really important, Maya. Take your time and truly embrace this exercise."

"Sounds good," Maya says, and takes one last look at her notes. She stands up and stretches again. "I'll see you in a bit."

"I'll be here ... watching over you like always!" giggles Michael.

"Creepy!" Maya laughs as she walks away.

MAYA'S NOTES ON EACH CHAKRA

chakra	Name	Colour	Seed Sound	Mantra
1	root chakra	red	LAM	I am safe, I am secure, I am rooted.
2	sacral chakra	orange	VAM	I am joy. I am divine creativity.
3	solar plexus chakra	yellow	RAM	I am gracefully powerful.
4	heart chakra	Green	YAM	I am love. I forgive myself. I forgive others.
5	throat chakra	light blue	HAM	I speak and hear clearly. I communicate with ease.
6	third eye chakra	indigo	AUM	I am intuitive. I see beyond the veil.
7	crown chakra	violet/ white	OM* silent	I am present. I am one.

MAYA'S MNEMONIC
DEVICES FOR MEMORY

Order of chakras— Rest so sweetly here throughout thin connection. Root, sacral, solar plexus, heart, throat, third eye, crown
Order of chakras— ROY-G(p)-BIV(w) Red, orange, yellow, green/pink, bright blue, indigo, violet/white
Order of seed sounds— Let vibrant rising young humans ascend open-heartedly LAM, VAM, RAM, YAM, HAM, AUM, ॐ OM

Maya finds a quiet place on the other side of the park to stand under the large branches of a majestic maple tree. She grounds to the earth and steps out under the sun to take in its energy and connect to Source. She begins to work through the chakras, releasing negative old energy that was stuck and inviting positive transformative energy into each chakra. Each time she chants a new seed sound and says a mantra, she feels lighter and fuller at the same time. Her body feels as though it is vibrating, unable to be contained in this small body. She feels her arms rise up as she reaches her crown chakra and realizes that she probably looks pretty silly in the park, but she washes away the negative thought quickly and embraces how amazing she feels. She is smiling with such powerful emotion that it feels as though her cheeks could burst. 'I am light.' she shouts in her mind. 'I am one! I've got this!'

Maya stands perfectly still for at least five minutes, sensing her surroundings. She can feel everything around her even though her eyes are closed. It is as if she sees everything as little bubbles, and the movement of one affects every single bubble around her. The blowing of a strand of hair in the wind sets off a chain reaction of movement that causes the wind to push a ladybug's flight path in a new direction. It lands on a young woman's face. Her boyfriend says, 'Make a wish,' as he lifts the ladybug off her face and releases it in the breeze with a light blow. This in turn signals to a bird to leave its nest. 'It's all connected,' Maya thinks. 'We are all connected! I get it! I truly get it!' She sits embracing this understanding a little longer, not sure if she will always feel this way or sense her surroundings like this as she moves forward. 'This feeling is like nothing she has ever felt. This knowing. How can it be possible?' The question sits on the tip of her tongue.

Source Energy reaches down to her mind. *It has always been so. You just weren't ready to hear it.*

'Thank you,' Maya thinks, 'I feel so blessed for knowing. For being allowed to open my heart and understanding to this knowledge.'

You have worked very hard this past week Maya. You are doing great. This next journey will prove difficult in many ways, but try to come back to this feeling, this knowing, any time that it feels too hard.

'I will,' Maya confirms. 'Thank you.'

Thank you, she hears. She stands quietly for another minute and then grounds herself back down through her chakras and into the earth. She opens her eyes and blinks at the sun.

'Hello Sun.' She smiles. 'Thank you for sharing your energy.' *Thank you,* she hears. 'Hello tree, hello Earth, thank you for sharing your energy.' She senses a return of gratitude. Maya starts to walk back to her blanket, thanking all of the things in her path for sharing their space and energy. When she arrives back to her blanket, she is radiating white light and positivity.

Michael is beaming, but waits patiently while she settles into her seat. She reaches for her bottle of water and takes a sip before feeling ready. "You have an amazing energy now!" he says.

Maya beams. "I feel amazing! Thank you for showing me how to do that!"

"It is always amazing, and often it can be different each time. Did you get any messages from Source?"

"Yes!" Maya tries to find the words. "It was a sense that we are all connected. I saw every object as a series of bubbles that become jostled around by each other. Each bubble carries an emotion that affects the next bubble. It was like a chain reaction."

"Yes! That's amazing, Maya!" Michael shouts. "Each cell carries our energy, and yes, it can look like little bubbles all vibrating at top speeds."

"Also," Maya continues, "I gave thanks for the information and to the sun, the trees, and the earth, and I received gratitude back."

"Yes!" confirms Michael. "The law of attraction again! That which you give—you receive!"

"Yes! That was super cool," Maya agrees, "but also, I kept giving gratitude on my walk back. I thanked the trees for their shade, strength, and beauty. I thanked the grass for its colour and home to many small insects. I thanked the flowers for their beauty and fragrance. I thanked the pathway for its guidance and space for everyone to walk. I thanked the people in the park for contributing their positive energy to the park. I thanked the builders of the park for creating such a beautiful space for the community to use. With each sentiment of gratitude, I felt even brighter and stronger. It was amazing!"

"That is the power!" says Michael. "I'm stoked that this is the message you received! That's awesome! Well, you are clearly brimming with positivity—let's get you set up for the next task."

"Okay," Maya starts, "so, I am going to ground, tune in, think of my location in time, and then ask the question of what do I need. Then as I am shifting and assimilating that knowledge, I need to project the idea that I am going somewhere else. Correct?"

"Exactly," confirms Michael.

DISTRACTION

"OKAY, YOU'RE GOING to try this tactic in three different ways," says Michael. "First, try to visit somewhere
you have already visited and then direct your energy to
another place that you also have already visited. Next, go
somewhere new that you haven't yet visited and direct
your energy to somewhere you have already been. Last, go
somewhere new and send your energy somewhere new.
This way you will have covered all of your bases."

"Great plan," says Maya. "Chat soon."

Maya grounds herself for her first attempt. She recalls
her visit to South Goa. She asks, 'What do I need to know
about this time-space reality?' Even though she has visited
Palolem before, she likes the idea that she may get to learn
something new and that she gets to practice this new
technique. She gets the sense that she should bring a towel
along as well. At the exact moment her intuition kicks
in, she shifts her thoughts to the Olympics in Mexico.
She envisions sending the Clippers to the base of the
torch. She arrives in Palolem Beach with a towel, ready
to swim, and she has to assume that her strategy worked.
She quickly runs into the water, dives in, and basks in the
sunshine. After she walks out and dries off with her towel,

she grounds herself again thinks about where she will go next. She needs to think of somewhere new while imagining sending the Clippers somewhere she has already been. She sits on her towel thinking for a few more minutes.

'I've got it!' Maya thinks. 'Brighton Beach, December twenty-fifth, 2003, eleven-fifteen a.m. 'What do I need to know about this time-space reality?' Maya quickly hears, *You're playing with fire ... and you know it! Keep your bathing suit and towel. Watch from afar.* As soon as Maya hears the warning, she thinks of the Calgary Stampede and visualizes the Clippers taking a detour. She arrives on the beach and looks up to see her mom in her twenties. She and her friends are celebrating Christmas on the beach. One of her male friends is barefoot and wearing a Santa hat. 'She looks so young and vibrant ... and fit!' Maya grins. 'Interesting that my intuition busted me for coming here ... Of course, I couldn't have done that if I was actually being chased. That would be way too dangerous. But one quick visit to see Mom in her youth couldn't hurt, could it?' Maya walks farther down the beach and chooses a place to sit and think where she can look back on her mom and her mom's friends.

This next shift will be a bit harder. She has to think of a new place and imagine sending the Clippers to a new place as well.

'Next up,' Maya thinks, 'City of Prague, June twenty-second, 1689, four p.m. What do I need to know about entering this time-space reality?' *Dress in dark, simple clothing. This is a sad day. Be prepared to see many terrible images. There was a devastating fire yesterday.* 'Oh,' Maya gasps and she tears up at the thought. She tries not to get distracted and visualizes sending the Clippers to April fifteenth, 1224, two fifty-three p.m.

She arrives in Prague to blackened streets punctuated by wails of utter heartbreak. She looks around, taking in the devastation. She realizes she feels different this time. She's not sure if it is because she has arrived somewhere in history that is so sad, or if the date she chose has somehow not worked out. She looks up the street at a family standing in front of their crumbled home, holding each other as they look on in disbelief.

She turns around and grounds. She thinks of home and what she was wearing when she started her journey. Maya opens her eyes to her comfortable blanket and weeps.

"Hey Maya," Michael says softly. "Are you okay? What happened?"

"It was awful," Maya heaves between sobs, wiping her nose with the sleeve of her jacket. "There was a terrible fire in Prague and the families were devastated."

"Oh, that is hard," Michael says, and waits for Maya's tears to slow before he continues. "Sometimes when we shift, we will see terrible things ... especially when we do not know the time-space reality that we are heading to. It cannot be helped. It is very hard not to be affected by it. The only advice I can give at this moment is to try to block out those emotions during our initiative and then afterward we can go back to these places and you can process the emotions that you had on first viewing. It does get easier as you learn to process emotions. I know that doesn't help when there are people who are hurting, but it becomes part of our journey."

"Yeah," Maya nods. "Maybe knowing that I can process everything when this is all over is a strategy to put off getting too upset during the journey."

"How did everything else go?" asks Michael.

"Mostly good," Maya says. "I have a few thoughts or questions."

"What's up?" Michael asks.

"Well," Maya starts, "The first trip was great; I went to Goa and imagined the Clippers in Mexico. Then I went to Brighton Beach and visualized the Clippers in Calgary. I was sort of warned or chastened by my intuition before arriving in Brighton Beach."

"Oh?" Michael raises an eyebrow. "Why's that?"

"Well," Maya said sheepishly, "I knew my mom would be celebrating Christmas on the beach with her friends and I thought it would be cool to see her when she was young. I got busted and told I was playing with fire."

"Yes." Michael agrees, "That could be very dangerous if you were being chased."

"I know." agrees Maya, "I would never do it while being chased; I just thought this was a great opportunity to check it—and her—out!"

"For sure." says Michael, "I get it, all of this is very exciting. I went looking for my parents when they were younger too. Many times, actually. Once, I spent an afternoon playing with my dad. He was about eight years old. We built a fort in the forest and pretended to be hunters. Coolest day ever!"

"What?" Maya laughs. "That's amazing!"

"It was pretty awesome! Maybe you will get to try that some day! But for now," Michael adds, "at least you have learned that lesson, and know to wait until this is all over. Visiting anyone you know is dangerous, but visiting your mom before you were born is particularly dangerous if the Pruner or the Clippers were to find out and search out a version of your mom before she had you. They could essentially negate your life and all of your experiences—including saving me!"

"Oh, my goodness, I hadn't even thought about that sort of thing! That is awful. I'm so sorry. I won't do that again, I promise." Maya says genuinely.

"It's okay. It's all new and I completely understand that you want to explore—I just want you to be safe at all times right now. Did anything of else of consequence happen during your travels?"

"Well, yes, one other thing ..." Maya continues. "On my last trip, when I was visualizing the Clippers going somewhere new, it was much harder to visualize because I didn't know where I was sending them."

"Right, no point of reference. That is difficult. So, what happened?"

"I'm not sure, but when I arrived in Prague, I had a different feeling. I am not sure if it was based on the calamity of the situation in Prague or the fact that maybe the Clippers would have found me on that shift."

"What does your intuition tell you?" asks Michael.

"It's telling me that I was just uncomfortable with the survivors of the fire. It says I need to have better faith next time that my intentions are working," Maya confirms.

"Perfect," Michael says. "This has been a very long day for you. You have done great. But I think it's time for a break. Take the night off and relax … let's aim to put the plan into action tomorrow when you're done school."

A NIGHT OFF

'A NIGHT OFF … what to do? Ask Mom to go out for dinner,' Maya thinks. She walks home grinning from ear to ear. 'It's truly amazing how much I have learned over the past few days. It's hard to believe that tomorrow we're really going to launch into this adventure. It has already felt like an adventure, but this is about to get a whole lot more real.' Maya takes a deep breath and sighs. 'It's funny how sighing can make a person feel so much better. I wonder why?' *Well, for starters, it relaxes your whole body. You can feel it in the way your shoulders relax down your back after a sigh. But also, it releases pent-up toxins that have been trapped in your cells.* Maya jumps, a little puzzled. *You wondered, I answered,* her intuition offered. Maya grins, 'So cool! Can you answer everything?' *No, not necessarily. Intuition can answer things that are directly related to your body or energy field. But only if you are open and ready for the information.* 'Still super awesome,' Maya smiles.

When Maya arrives home, she bursts through the door, super excited to see her mom. 'Hi mom!' she yells, waiting for a response. Her mom isn't home. Maya decides to sit down and make her mom a card. A gratitude card for taking her out to dinner, 'She'll eat that up!' Maya thinks.

She grabs some paper and markers out of the storage bin beside the table, and folds the paper in half. She chooses three bright colours because she likes her artwork to be colour coordinated. Bright blue, pink, and green. Maya ponders what to say, and then starts writing. *Mom. You are the bestest, most super mom in the world. I'd love to have an evening out with you—please take us out for dinner! Your most favourite (and only) daughter. Maya.* 'Perfect,' Maya grins, and starts adding designs around the outside.

Maya leaves the card on the kitchen table and runs upstairs to shower. As she is getting ready for her shower, she hears her mom come in the back door.

"Honey! I'm home!" Mom calls.

Three … two … one." Maya whispers and grins.

"Awe, you made me a card!" Mom reads the card silently, smiling.

"I'm just hopping in the shower!" Maya waits a few seconds, then turns on the water. As soon as she has climbed into the shower, the bathroom door opens.

"You want to go for dinner, love?" Mom asks.

"Yes, pleeeeease!" Maya croons.

"Sure thing! Let's do something fancy. Let's go to that artisan pizzeria downtown, at the bottom of Main Street. We can get all dolled up!" Mom almost sings.

"Sounds amazing, Mom!" Maya smiles, her heart full.

Maya takes a long, enjoyable shower, releasing the tension of sitting all day. Then she towels off in the unplanned steam room. She turns on the fan and walks out of the bathroom, leaving the door open to help air it out. Maya walks past her mom's room on her way to get dressed. "Shower's free!"

"Thanks, honey!" her mom calls from inside her walk-in closet. "Just picking out an outfit."

Maya loves when her mom gets dressed up. It doesn't happen often. Usually, she just wears yoga pants and baggy sweaters. It's fun when they get fancy together too, it's like a ritual—the hair, the make-up, chatting about their day.

Maya chooses a turquoise blue dress that can be on or off the shoulders. It has a brown leather belt that loops around the waist. She looks for a sweater that will work with the dress and sets out a pair of white sandals. She walks into the bathroom where her mom has just stepped out of the shower and is towel drying her hair, and she starts to brush out her hair while grinning at her mom in the mirror.

"Would you like me to blow it out for you?" Mom asks.

'I knew she would.' Maya thinks, and nods.

Mom gives her a squeeze and says, "You're getting so big. I love you so much."

"Thanks, Mom." Maya squirms. "I love you too!"

They spend the next twenty minutes beautifying. Maya watches her mom do her make-up routine and blow dry her own hair. 'I wonder why I can't dry my hair as easily.' Maya thinks. *It's a skill; you are learning. Be patient with yourself.* Maya grins at her intuition. Then Mom takes an extra hand towel and dries out the lengths of Maya's hair, squeezing the excess water into the towel. As her mom dries her hair, Maya watches her more closely in the mirror. 'She really is beautiful. I love her so much," Maya thinks. Then she says out loud, "Mom, you are amazing!"

Mom laughs. "Thank you darling, I try!" She flips a piece of hair over her shoulder in a big to-do, and reaches down and tickles Maya's tummy. Maya turns and hugs her, tighter than she meant to. Her mom turns off the blow dryer and hugs her back, kissing the top of her head.

"I love you, baby. You okay?" Mom asks.

"Yes." Maya sniffles. "I just need this night with you."

"Thanks, love." Mom says, "I think we both need it!"

Mom finishes drying Maya's hair and puts the hairdryer back in its drawer. She kisses her again on the top of her head and walks out to get dressed. Maya follows her and sits on her bed. Her mom comes out in a black sundress with a big chunky turquoise necklace and black sandals.

"Look," she said, "We'll match a bit! Did you choose a necklace?"

"Oh, I forgot!" Maya exclaims. She runs back to her room and grabs the rose-quartz pendant. It was her mom's. She had borrowed it a long time ago and her mom had never seemed to mind. She unclips it as she walks back into her mom's room, and holds it up to her neck as she turns away from her mom so that she can help her clip it at the back.

Mom spins her around and grabs her hands. Stretching out, they look at each other. "Perfect!" Mom winks. "Let's go!"

They walk down the street to the main drag. It is a lovely night. There aren't a lot of tourists here this weekend, which is strange for this time of year. It makes the street calmer than usual. When they arrive at the restaurant, a table is waiting for them. 'Mom must have called while I was in the shower,'

Maya thinks. 'We got our favourite table by the window.' The giant bay windows are open, letting in a soft breeze from off the bay. Everything feels perfect. They share a Caesar salad, the spice-rubbed ribs, and a Pompeii pizza with pancetta and pineapple. The servers are amazing, as always. They know Mom; this is her favourite restaurant. They do this cool trick with olive oil and salt where you dip your crusts. It is truly delicious. Maya and her mom chat the whole time, joking, laughing, and sharing new goals. It is a wonderful evening.

Afterward, they walk down by the waterfront to look at the sunset and grab an ice cream cone. They sit on one of the benches near the docks and watch the seagulls spin and dart around the sky. Maya reaches out to hold her mom's hand. They sit quietly, licking their ice cream. 'This moment,' Maya thinks, 'This night, is one to remember … to keep me content for a long time.'

When they finish their ice cream they walk home, arms linked, chatting about some of the mundane things coming up in their lives. Maya was only partially paying attention and agreeing, knowing that her life was about to change drastically.

When they get home, Maya hugs her mom and goes straight to her room to read for a few minutes. She falls asleep while reading.

Mom sneaks in and lifts Maya's book out of her hands, "Good night, sweet girl." She kisses Maya on the forehead and turns off the light.

EXECUTE

MAYA WAKES UP early, feeling content and refreshed. She grins and jumps out of bed, ready to start this day. She runs into her mom's room and jumps on the bed. "Good morning!" She squeals. Her mom groans. "I have a really big day today, Mom. Can you please make me pancakes while I hop in the shower?" Maya jumps up and bounces twice before running off to the bathroom. 'It might be the last shower I take for a while!' Maya thinks.

When Maya gets out of the shower, she can hear her mom whisking batter in the kitchen. She smiles. 'She's so good to me. I need to remember to be more grateful when I return to this time-space reality ... Well, I guess I need to just start being more grateful every day! For everything!' Maya prompts herself.

Maya puts on her usual jeans and a nondescript T-shirt and heads downstairs. "Thanks, Mom!" She kisses her cheek, grabs a plate, and loads up a few pancakes with butter and syrup.

"Grab some fruit too, kid!" Mom scolds.

"I'm going to pack some in my lunch." Maya muffles between mouthfuls.

"Sounds good." Mom says. "Have a great day. I'm going back to bed."

"Wait!" Maya yells, and swallows her food hard. She jumps up and hugs her mom as tight as she can. She takes a deep breath and takes in her mom's scent, trying to commit it to memory. "I love you."

"I love you too, babe!" Mom replies. "See you this evening."

Maya nods, wondering when *this evening* might actually become a reality. She sits back down and gobbles her breakfast. After she finishes, she clears her dishes and starts to pack a lunch for school and snacks for the journey. Choices are limited if she were to get caught … she can't have plastic bags or containers. She grabs a few cloth beeswax wraps out of the cupboard … at least she could explain cloth somehow if she had to. She packs nuts, apples, pepperettes, and granola bars without their packaging.

On her walk to school, she starts noticing everything and giving gratitude. 'Thank you for the sunshine that gives warmth to my face and nutrients to plants. Thank you for the sidewalk for a safe place to walk. Thank you to the street signs that show me where to go. Thank you to the architect who designed such beautiful houses. Thank you to the gardeners for arranging beauty in their yards. Thank you to the flowers for sharing their beauty.' Maya continues like this with each thing she sees. By the time she gets to school, she is beaming. A few classmates smile at her as she walks past, humming in her contentment.

School feels just as long today as it did yesterday, but the energy is a bit different. Today is the day. Today it gets real. Maya holds onto a slight twinge of nerves as she thinks about her pending journey. She decides to let it go and think only of gratitude throughout her day.

When the final bell rings, Maya thoughtfully packs up her things and swings by her locker to drop off her school supplies and pick up her travel snacks. She chats to a few friends in the hallway, giving them compliments on their hair or clothing and hugging them goodbye. It's funny, Maya would never have hugged them last week, but today this feels completely normal … and they hug back as if it is normal as well.

Her walk from school to the park is short, but Maya brings herself back to gratitude on her walk. Thanking the tennis courts for providing a place to be active. Thanking the post office for delivering good news to the citizens. Thanking the kind folks at the fire department for their service in keeping the town safe.

By the time she lays out her blanket in the park, she is beaming again.

"Taking a gratitude walk I see," says Michael.

"They are so amazing, Michael!" Maya beams. "I feel energized!"

"That's great, Maya!" Michael responds. "On that note, I want to thank you."

"Me?" asks Maya.

"Yes! You!" says Michael emphatically. "In the end, I'm not really sure what is going to happen, and I am extremely grateful for your contributions, Maya. Your unwavering faith that you will be able to save not only me, but the world from this threat." Michael bows his head in prayer pose. "Namaste."

"Namaste …" Maya rolls the word on her lips. "My mom says that a lot. I don't really know what it means, but I do know that when one person says it, usually the other person responds with the same word. What does it mean exactly?"

"Well, at its most basic level, it is a greeting or a form of gratitude," Michael defines. "It's a Sanskrit word. Namaskar is the act of bowing or respecting something, where Namaste is the idea of bowing to you. If you look at more in-depth definitions, the two most common phrases that surround Namaste are, 'The Divine in me bows to the Divine in you.' Or more expansively, 'I recognize and honour the Divine light in you just as you recognize and honour the Divine light in me.' Essentially, it's saying I honour the light and love within you just as it is within me because we are both equal and we are all part of the one greater collective light and energy."

Maya's eyes widen with a look of disbelief. "Wow … that is so cool!" she exclaims. "My mom is actually quite deep!"

"Yeah, she seems pretty cool, Maya!" Michael agrees. "Well, if you're ready, check your surroundings for when you come back."

"Yes, I am!" Maya sighs and giggles, "That felt like an affirmation I would do with my mom!"

"No way!" Michael laughs. "Ooh, affirmations are so great! What sort of affirmations would you do with her?"

"Every morning when I was little," Maya remembers, "She would say an affirmation and have me repeat it to her. Phrases like, 'I am strong. I am kind. I choose to make it a great day. Today I grow my brain. I've got this, Mama.' If there was something in particular that was bothering me, she would add that in for a few days as well until it cleared."

"That's amazing Maya!" Michaels grins. "It's as if you were being groomed for this role and your mom didn't even know it!"

"Fate? Divine timing? Who knows? It worked!" Maya shrugs.

"Definitely!" agrees Michael. "Okay, what are you coming back to?"

Maya looks around the park. It is another calm day. She wonders why there aren't a lot of people visiting this week. She spots a family with three children. The mom is pushing a baby in the swing. She is wearing a flowery scarf that is blowing in the wind. The baby is wearing a yellow onesie with blue shorts. The two older children, maybe three and five, are running around the slide area, their dad chasing them. The older girl is climbing the wooden structure to get up to the slide while the little boy waits, holding the wooden rails. "Uppie," he calls to his dad and motions his hands upward. Maya looks at her watch, two twenty-two p.m. May tenth, 2022.

"Wow! That's a lot of twos!" she says, after having described the scene to Michael.

"Very auspicious!" Michael agrees. "Seeing repeated twos is a sign of universal support for unity and collaboration. So cool!"

Maya is taken aback. "That is amazing! It makes me feel even better—like all of this is meant to be happening!"

"I agree," Michael says. "There are just so many positive things happening here, it's hard not to believe we are meant to be going through this together! Okay, get comfortable and take a couple breaths while I walk you through the day … To start, I'm going to set up a protective energy field around you that will both help keep you safe and will hopefully be able to magnify your message. Then, we will sit and build your energy from here together. Once you feel ready, you can make your first shift. When you arrive, connect in like you've practiced and open your awareness to your whole field so that you can sense if any Clippers come near you. Then start the Mayday call. If at any time you sense the Clippers—shift to your next location immediately, setting blocks and sending the Clippers to an alternate location. Don't even open your eyes or look around, just shift and begin again. If you never feel them, great! Then keep going! You've done amazing so far. I have complete faith in you, Maya!" Michael boasts, "I'm sending you as much loving energy as I can and I will stay here once you leave and hold space for you for as long as I can."

"Amazing! Thank you. For everything." Maya is near tears. "I'll see you soon, Michael."

"Maya," Michael pauses. "I love you. I love your energy. I love your contribution. You've got this!"

"I've got this!" Maya sniffles.

"Try this." Michael adds. "Rub your hands together fast, about ten times."

Maya starts to rub her hands together.

"Now put your hands over your eyes and wipe up over your hair and down the back of your head like you are rinsing water through your hair," Michael guides.

Maya does this, and immediately feels lighter.

"Good," Michael continues. "Do that two more times and then let out a big sigh."

Maya does the rub and rinse two more times and lets out a giant relaxing sigh. "Wow!" she says. "You have all these great tricks to raise my vibration and help me stay focused. How will I do this without you?"

"Correction." Michael stops her, "You have all these great tricks at your fingertips … ready for you. Everything I have taught you is available to you at any time. Plus, if you ask your intuition what you need at the moment, you will inherently know!"

"Right!" Maya nods. "I need to remember to do this!"

"Think of it this way," Michael expands, "when you get scared and wonder what would I do, think of me saying, 'Ask yourself!'"

Maya laughs. "Thank you, that is a great plan. I'll feel like you are right there with me!"

"Maya," Michael pauses until Maya seems ready, "It's time."

Maya nods and centres herself.

"Here we go." Michael begins, "Take a deep inhale, and exhale with a sigh. Take another inhale, exhale with a sigh, inhale, exhale and sigh. Now let yourself breathe normally, cleansing each breath as you inhale through the nose, exhaling and releasing anything that no longer serves you."

Maya sighs loudly on the last exhale and her shoulders drop as she sinks into a comfortable rhythm. She is lulled by Michael's voice.

"Take this time to imagine a white ball of glowing energy at your heart centre. Inhale, I am love, exhale, we are love. See this ball of energy taking up your whole heart; feel this energy growing with each inhale so that it encompasses your whole body. Feel your vibration rising as you do this. Now envision this energy moving down through your solar plexus chakra, down through your sacral chakra, and into your root chakra. Feel it travel down through your hips, legs, knees, ankles, and feet. Feel the energy root you to the ground as it travels further toward the centre of earth. Take in the earth's nutrients and life force energy.

"Inhale all the way back up to your feet, up through the lower chakras and into your heart chakra again. Now envision the energy rising up through your throat chakra, up through your third eye chakra, and up to your crown chakra. This energy is travelling up from your crown chakra to Source Energy. Inhale energy down from Source through your upper chakras, back through your heart chakra. Do this a few more times, exhale into the earth releasing that which does not serve you to be transmuted into light, inhale life force energy from the earth. Exhale energy to the Source, inhale Source Energy back down to you, completing the circle."

Michael pauses, allowing Maya to complete a couple more cycles on her own.

"Now think of this energy as a growing ball of light, consuming your six-foot energy field. With each inhale, the light and energy continue to grow, they contain your whole block, your whole city, your whole country, the whole earth, the whole universe. Sit in this expansive energy until you are ready." Michael sits quietly and waits.

Maya takes a few more breaths. She feels safe, cocooned by Michael, the earth, and Source Energy. Her vibration is strong and she is beaming energy out from her heart centre. Maya shifts to the beaches of Goa, believing in her heart that she is safe and that she will only need one location and one attempt to make the Mayday call. As she shifts, she asks, 'Is there anything I need to know about entering this time-space reality?' She heard back, loud and clear, *You already know all you need to know in this time-space reality.* Maya directs her attention to the Calgary Stampede, hoping that she does not yet need this sort of distraction.

Maya arrives at Palolem Beach and sets out her towel. She is still very much engaged with the energy that she and Michael have set up. She sits down and immediately sets intentions. Maya's intention is to only reach light-workers and beings with the highest intentions. She calls all archangels to support this message. Calling the arch-angel Raphael and the Element of Air to protect the East. Calling in the archangel Michael and the Element of Fire to protect the South. Calling in the archangel Gabriel and the Element of Water to protect the West, and calling in the archangel Uriel and the Element of Earth to protect the North.

Next, Maya calls in her personal team of any other archangels, ancestors, descendants, and all fellow light-workers. Then she sets the intention that the Pruner, the Clippers, and any of their allies are blocked from her thoughts.

Maya begins to focus on her heart centre, allowing light to fill her body and taking a few deep breaths to reconnect to the earth's core and Source Energy. With each inhale, Maya calls in more and more light, and with each exhale she sends out love and light to the universe. She continues to say, "I am Light, Creator bring me light. Creator, I am Light, give me light." Now that she is radiating at her full potential, Maya restates the intention that the message is only for beings of highest intention and that any commu-nication about this topic will be blocked from the senses of the Pruner and the Clippers.

'GO time,' Maya thinks, and begins the scariest journey of her life!

"Mayday, Mayday, Mayday. Time is short. We are in grave danger. The Pruner is sending Clippers to steal your internal clocks and take away your ability to connect. We must STOP them immediately. All available lightworkers are to generate shields of light. Invite and teach as many people as possible. Protect yourselves and set up blocks for yourself and the community as often as needed. Call in all archangels, light consciousness, ancestors, and descendants of the highest vibration. Travel fast and light. Collaborate and send healing energy to all those light beings affected. Send loving light energy to the Pruner himself, and all of his allies. He was one of ours. Turned. We need solutions to solve or transmute this problem. Who has ideas?"

After waiting a minute, Maya begins again, infusing love into the Mayday message, "Mayday, Mayday, Mayday. Time is short. We are in grave danger. The Pruner is sending Clippers to steal your internal clocks and take away your ability to connect. We must STOP them immediately. All available lightworkers are to generate shields of light. Invite and teach as many people as possible. Protect yourselves and set up blocks for yourself and the community as often as needed. Call in all archangels, light consciousness, ancestors, and descendants of the highest vibration. Travel fast and light. Collaborate and send healing energy to all those light beings affected. Send loving light energy to the Pruner himself, and all of his allies. He was one of ours. Turned. We need solutions to solve or transmute this problem. Who has ideas?"

Almost immediately, Maya starts seeing light beings come into her field of consciousness. Gradually, more and more beings appear. She feels their presence and sees their light in her field of vision. They are teaming up to create a circle of lightworkers around her ... each seemingly magnifying her light and message. The intensity of the colours is breathtaking. White, indigo, blue, green, yellow, orange, red, and pink. She feels a surge of energy ground down through to the earth's core and immediately climb back to her crown chakras and up into the sky. The light travels with each breath up to the heavens and outward down to the earth ... each breath brings more lightworkers to her field of energy. She is still no closer to an idea. Doubt begins to creep in.

Just then a gentle soul seems to grab her metaphorical hand. "You are safe, Maya. We are finding the answer. Stay with the light. Feel the light. You are acting as a vortex, pulling in all of the light beings of the universe. We need you to be grounded and feel safe."

Maya immediately feels relaxed. She relaxes deeper and starts to enjoy the light show. Each energetic being entering presents as a different tint of colour. As Maya watches, she starts to realize there is an energetic pattern happening all around them. The crossing of energies is creating a dome around her. She wonders what it is. *It's the Flower of Light.* 'What's the Flower of Light?' Maya asks. *It's a design in sacred geometry.* 'What does sacred geometry mean?' *There are some perfect shapes that are believed to be the template of all life. The Flower of Life represents the unity of all things.* 'It's so beautiful.'

Maya watches the experience as if she is on the outside. She feels as though she has joined up with her destiny. It feels a bit like a reunion. Light beings are giving her metaphorical high fives as they enter and join the circle. Each one brings in more light, more colour, and more energy. All of a sudden, the voice that calmed her starts speaking to everyone.

"It is time ... everyone ... take an in-breath altogether," the voice says. Maya can feel a huge influx of energy as the whole Collective inhales. "Now exhale love into Mother Earth ... Inhale loving white light from Source Energy, and exhale, expanding your energy field. Inhale loving white light and exhale loving energy to the world. Inhale loving white light energy and exhale directly to the Pruner. Again! Inhale loving white light energy and exhale loving energy to the Pruner. Again! Continue in the pattern. Inhale. Exhale. Inhale. Exhale. Inhale. Exhale.

"Whew! Feel that, everyone! You're rocking it! Everyone, in-breath and out-breath to the whole situation. Inhale. Exhale. Inhale loving energy. Exhale to all those souls hurt in the process of pruning. Again! Continue this pattern! Inhale. Exhale. Inhale. Exhale. And hold. Hold that energy. Radiate love to all things in all time-space realities."

The Collective pulses. The energy moves in waves as if magnetized by their communal efforts. The ebb and flow of energy magnifies with each breath. More and more power is coming to the Collective to share with the universe. As Maya sits in the middle of this process, she begins to see each light being and every particle of matter as little bubbles. With each inhale, the bubbles fill with white light, and with each exhale bubbles are sent off into the universe to spread love and joy.

As the energy grows, Maya starts to feel the Pruner and the Clippers getting closer. She starts to feel worried about what might happen. She wonders if she should change locations. She fears losing her internal clock. She worries about her mom, and quickly remembers she wasn't supposed to think about that.

Just then, a woman, at least Maya thinks it's a woman, kindly says in a thick accent, "Calm your mind, child, you are safe. Stay here with us now. Focus solely on the positive. Take a deep breath." Maya obeys. She takes the deepest breath she can manage. She sighs and breathes in again slowly.

"Negative self-talk is the surest way to self-destruct, and more importantly, the Community will crumble if you don't hold space for this message."

"It's crazy how you can all pick up on my thoughts," Maya thinks.

"We will teach you many things, all in good time my dear. All in good time," the woman assures Maya.

Even though Maya continues to feel the negative presence grow, she keeps holding space for positive, loving energy. She knows that even as it gets closer, the Collective is winning. Their light is emitting at such a great rate that there will be no way to overcome them.

While they are not in the same location as the Pruner, his image all of a sudden appears in their sight. Their light begins penetrating his bodily form from all directions. He is trying to fight it; he is trying to set up blocks against them, but the Collective is too powerful. A flicker of light begins to grow in the Pruner's root chakra.

"Nooo! the Pruner yells. "This can't be happening!"

The flicker quickly becomes a flame of light and continues to grow. As it struggles against the Pruner's attempts to block it, the light begins to climb up to his sacral chakra, gaining speed and light. As the light and energy reaches his solar plexus chakra, it appears as if the Pruner's body is beginning to fill with up with liquid light emanating out from the three lower chakras. When it reaches his heart chakra, the light begins to pulsate. The light begins to grow stronger, brighter, and more encompassing of the Pruner's body. It then climbs up into his throat, third eye, and crown chakras. As the last of the seven chakras lights up, a sphere of light encompasses the whole energetic bubble of the Pruner.

The Community continues to send love and light to all of the cells contained within the bubble. The sphere begins to pulsate faster, expanding and contracting with each breath of the Collective. The Pruner's body appears to lift off the ground, as if weightless within his bubble. The cleansing energy of the light and love brightening with each breath. Suddenly, the Pruner's bubble expands beyond its bubble, almost as if it explodes into tiny shards of light, tiny bubbles that scatter throughout the sky, sprinkling love and light everywhere. It is miraculous. It is almost as if there is a giant firework set off above the Collective, sparkling through the Flower of Light. The overwhelming love that radiates on the community surges. Even though they are all sitting peacefully in different time-space realities, it is as if they are all accomplices in the single-most important life event they would ever witness. It feels as if there were no Ages, no time-space realities. There is no separation. They are all one. They silently celebrate their great success. The Collective continues to radiate love and light, basking in the positivity and awaiting their next instruction.

THE SEARCH
BEGINS

"FOCUS, EVERYONE!" A gentle male voice says. "We have just had a major breakthrough, but there is still much to do. Keep this energy high and hold space for the Clippers. We still need to find and heal all of the Clippers, the Pruner's allies, and the Pruner's victims. We need to try to find anyone who has lost their internal clock and start figuring out if there is a way to find the clocks and heal these Community members. We also need to search for the machine that the Pruner was using to hurt our Community members and destroy it."

The voice now switches from giving directive messages to the Collective to searching the Collective.

"Michael? Michael? ... Are you there? Michael?"

"You know Michael?" Maya interjects.

"Yes! I need to find him. Have you seen him? Or spoken to him?" the voice asks.

"Yes!" Maya laughs nervously. "I've been speaking with him every day."

"Where is he?" asks the voice, near panic.

"I don't know exactly. He says it's like no place he has ever been before." Maya responds.

"You haven't been there?" the voice questions.

"No, he can speak to me, but he can't shift. He said that his internal clock was removed," Maya answers.

"Oh." the voice pauses in shock. "How did he connect with you if his internal clock is removed?"

"I'm not really sure." Maya confesses. "It only works from my home, unless we have planned a specific place. He said that it would be dangerous to return home during this mission, and to have a specific meeting place would put my family and me at risk."

"That is true, but the worst of it is gone. If we go in a group to your time-space reality, we can set up lookouts for the Clippers while the Collective continues to sending healing energy," he says.

"Um, okay; one question. Who are you?" Maya asks.

"Oh, my goodness, I am so sorry!" he says. "I'm Gabe."

"Gabe?" Maya questions.

"What?" Gabe chuckles. "Michael didn't tell you about his charming older brother?"

"Oh," Maya laughs. "He did, I just didn't catch your name! That's amazing! What do you need to meet me in my time-space reality?"

"We need backup! One sec …" Gabe turns his attention back to the Collective. "Maya and I are going to meet up in the physical realm to try to save my brother. Are there any of you who want to join us for protection and to help us look for other missing community members? It would also be useful if we take at least one healer."

Immediately the vibration of "Yes!" is felt as five light beings step forward. "Let's go save Michael and the others!"

"Amazing!" Gabe shouts. "Everyone else … stay connected and continue to hold space. Can I delegate you, Haylen, to hold space and continue guiding the group through inhalations and exhalations?"

Haylen nods. She discreetly takes over guiding the group meditation.

"Thank you," Gabe bows to Haylen's presence. "Where to, Maya?"

"Are we going to my current time-space reality?" Maya wonders.

"Yes!" Gabe confirms. "And all seven of us will meet there and tap into Michael through you."

"Sounds good," Maya says. "Two twenty-two p.m. May tenth, 2022. Walter Henry Park, West Ridge, Orillia. Canada."

"All right, people. Sync in and I'll hug you soon! Set up protection as soon as you arrive to camouflage our space!" Gabe adds.

"Camouflage?" asks Maya.

"No worries, Maya." Gabe notes. "We can set this up when we arrive, and I will teach you later. You don't need to be camouflaged because it is your home and you will be reconnecting with yourself."

"Okay. Perfect. See you soon." Maya grounds and shifts home.

HOME

MAYA ARRIVES BACK in the park, and is standing in a circle of smiling faces. She did not expect to be home this soon and falls into Gabe's arms nearly in tears. Gabe is about 16 or 17. He has dark brown, almost black, hair. His jawbone is strong and angular. His arms wrap around Maya and soothe her.

"You did great, Maya! A true rock star!" He steps back a bit and looks into her eyes. "The worst is likely over, but we are far from done. Can you still be strong?"

"Yes," Maya nods and wipes her tears. "I'm sorry. I didn't expect to react this way."

"You never need to be sorry about emotions, Maya," Gabe encourages her. "Emotions are the only true equalizer on this earth. You need to allow them to come and let them be released. Never push them aside or they will fester. Take a moment to feel through them and release them."

Maya wipes her eyes and sits quietly for a minute, taking deep inhalations and exhalations. After a few breaths, her body intuitively relaxes. She pauses and looks around with a disbelieving smile.

"Wow. What an amazing feeling!"

"Pretty cool, eh?" Gabe agrees.

"Very!" Maya exhales again.

"Are you ready?" Gabe asks.

"Yup; I feel much better. Thank you for giving me space," Maya smiles.

"You got it! No worries. Okay, let's meet your team!" Gabe holds his hand out to the group.

The first gentleman steps forward. He is older, but not old. Close to her mom's age, but a bit younger—maybe forty. He has a long beard and is wearing a cloak of sorts.

"My name is Klaus," he says in a German accent. "I am happy to be here to help."

"Thank you," Maya says, nodding, nearly bowing, and turns to the next person.

The woman is older than Klaus, but not by much. She has similar flaming red hair like Maya's but her eyes are steely blue.

"Hello, Maya," she says in the sweetest Scottish accent—the voice from the meditation—she reaches for Maya's hands. She looks deep into Maya's eyes and says, "My name is Maeve. You are a brave, brave girl. You have done well and I am so proud of you."

"Thank you." Maya beams.

The next person is much younger than the first two, but still an adult. Maybe in his early twenties. He is quite tall, taller than everyone else, and his hair is buzzed short all around. He kneels down before Maya so that she could look directly into his eyes. His eyes are dark brown, even darker than his skin, and they smile in the light. He reaches out and pulls Maya into a hug.

"You are a gem, my friend; you have saved many people, and I will always support you whenever and wherever you need it." he says in a much gruffer voice than she expected. "My name is Isaac."

"Thank you." Maya says and hugs him back. "Much appreciated."

The fourth person is also a young man, and likely in his late twenties or early thirties. He has short blonde hair, buzzed around the edges with a small tuft on top that hangs forward around his forehead. His eyes are caramel brown and emit a calm shyness. He takes a step forward.

"Hello Maya, I'm Pax," he says in a soft voice.

"Hi Pax," Maya smiles. "Thanks for coming!"

He grins, blushes, and steps back to his place in the circle.

The last of the five volunteers looks like a petite teenager with black eyes and long, jet-black hair. She steps forward and bows.

"*Konnichiwa*, my name is Shoko. I am happy to be here."

"Thank you so much!" Maya says, and bows in return.

"Well, now that you have met everyone, can we call in Michael?" Gabe asks excitedly.

"Oh," Maya says, a bit stunned. "He's probably already here. I got so distracted by all of you!" Maya redirects her attention inward. "Michael, are you there?"

"I'm here," Michael says, depleted.

"Are you okay?" asks Gabe.

Maya looks at Gabe with a sense of questioning, "How can you hear him?"

"I'm not sure," Gabe shrugs. "It's like you are a portal for Michael."

"Portal?" Maya questions.

Gabe holds up a finger, gesturing that the question could wait and redirects, "Michael, are you okay?"

"It's definitely getting worse. There is less food each week. I'm tingling all over. It's weird. My head is itchy, it's tingling so much! And my legs. Why am I tingling so much, Gabe?" Michael implores.

"I don't know, brother," says Gabe. "We're going to try to get you out of there. Can you communicate your location?"

"I don't know, Gabe," Michael pauses, seeming to look around at his surroundings. "It's like I am nowhere. There is no feeling here. No life. I can't get a grasp of the time-space reality."

"Okay. We'll try a different tactic; hold on," Gabe says, turning to all of us. "We need more information. I think we need to seek out the home base or headquarters of the Pruner to see if we can figure out where he is sending everyone after he takes out their internal clocks."

"We could also try to find some of the Clippers who are raising their vibration and see if they can give us more details, or direct us to the headquarters," adds Klaus.

"True," responds Gabe. "Michael, we are going to shift to a different time-space reality. We will come back to come find you when we have more details!"

"Sounds good, brother, be safe, and take care of my girl Maya!" Michael adds.

"We will! I know she is the powerhouse in this situation." Gabe ruffles Maya's hair.

Maya looks up and giggles. "Where will we go now, Gabe?"

WHAT'S NEXT?

GABE LOOKS TO the rest of the circle.

"Do any of you have a suggestion of where we can set up a circle of safety to begin our search and use as a home base until we find more concrete information?"

"*Hai*," says Shoko. "There is a great market in Takayama each morning. We can meet at the end of the bridge, in front of the red brick building. Shall we say ten a.m., April fifteenth, 2017?"

"Sounds good. When you arrive, remember to set up camouflage again." Gabe turns to the group.

"Gabe," Maya interrupts, "is this a good time to learn how to camouflage?"

"Yes, Maya!" exclaims Gabe. "I'm so sorry; I completely forgot! It's really quite simple. When you arrive at a location where you want to be camouflaged, you simply need to set the intention that you are camouflaged. You can also imagine yourself wearing all black, as often wearing black makes you 'unseen' in society."

"Oh, okay," says Maya, and adds, "That's simple enough, but you are all camouflaged now and you're not wearing black; why is that?"

"Great question." adds Maeve. "For starters, it's all in your head. You just need to imagine it, and so it is. Your belief is strong, and you can make whatever you believe a reality. Second, some of us are imagining we are in black, others hold the faith in their intention to not be seen. You are welcome to try either, but we would recommend that you imagine wearing black to begin, so that you are extra safe." She smiles endearingly.

"Got it!" Maya confirms. "Let's get this show on the road."

MEETING PLACE

WITHIN SECONDS THEY arrive in the same circular formation at the end of the bridge.

"Great job, Maya!" Isaac smiles. "You're doing great!"

Maya smiles shyly. "What now?" she asks.

"We are going to connect into the Collective and set the intention to find the Pruner's headquarters or any Clippers that can help direct us." Gabe begins, and turns to the group. "How do you feel about splitting up? Do we want to divide and conquer, or do we feel safer travelling together?"

"I think we need to stay together at this point. With only six of us to set a barrier around Maya, I think we are stronger together and will likely accomplish more in unison, even though that feels contradictory." Klaus notes.

"I'm good with that." says Gabe. "So, if anything goes wrong, immediately come here to meet, arrive camouflaged and ready to wait for everyone. If for some reason one of us cannot make it back, try to send that message to the Collective. If ... once you are here, someone is missing, tap into the Collective to see if there is a message, or to call on another light being to come in as a protector."

"Question." Maya raises her hand, and then laughs sheepishly as she lowers it. "How will I see you if you are all camouflaged when I get back?"

"Intention, Maya," says Shoko. "Everything we do is based on intention. As you are camouflaging, set the intention that we, or any light beings that can help us, can see you."

Maya grins, a bit embarrassed. "I'm starting to understand how much impact intention has in this situation!"

"In all situations." Pax adds.

The whole group connects into the Collective. Gabe continues to be the voice of the group. He asks general questions of the Collective, searching for energy that needs healing and Clippers who have already started their healing and growth journey that can help them find the Pruner's headquarters.

There is a ripple of energy that begins moving throughout the Collective. It surges toward the small group, encompassing their circle. It begins to loop and tug at the group, urging them to follow. Gabe verbally sets the intention that together, they will follow this energy to its helpful conclusion. Maya feels the circle begin to move. The circle formation stays intact and protected, like a cocoon, and they move as one unit. Their energy seems to spin them into a tunnel. The tunnel takes them faster and farther, deeper down the tunnel. Farther and farther along they go.

"What's happening?" asks Maya.

165

"We are being guided to a specific location, which will likely be either the Pruner's headquarters or a being that can help guide us there," Maeve tells her in a near whisper.

After a few more minutes on this tumultuous path, the group is almost spit out of the tunnel. They arrive in their circular formation in a courtyard, framed by lush plants, or rather overgrown plants. The green vines spiral up and around the wrought iron fence posts. The vines on the gate at the end of the courtyard look as if they had recently been cut back. There are flower pots that hold a variety of fruits and vegetables. The circle settles and sets camouflage as a precaution. They look around, taking in their surroundings.

Gabe looks to Maya and says, "Take a few extra moment to ground and settle yourself in this time-space reality. That was a long journey; we have come a long way and this trip has been very hard on our bodies. Take some deep breaths and let yourself feel grounded."

Maya nods and takes a few deep breaths.

The circle disperses a bit as each protector explores the courtyard.

"Look over here," Pax notices, pointing north toward an open doorway leading inside a building.

"Okay, everyone," Gabe says, "circle up. Let's move cautiously and stay on guard."

The group moves toward the entrance of the building, collapsing their circle to pass through the doorway, keeping Maya in the centre of their energy and protection. Klaus goes first. Maya notices he is armed with a sword that is hanging beneath his cloak. While he appears ready for action, he does not reach for the hilt, but rather he leads with a calm confidence that everything will be okay. He looks both ways as he enters, then steps to the right. Isaac follows Klaus, ducking as he steps through and to the left. Both men survey the interior. It is a large, empty foyer with marble walls, slate grey floors, and an interior door in the centre of each wall.

"Hello?" calls Klaus. His voice echoes through the foyer and into the outlying rooms. No one answers. The group moves further into the foyer and heads toward the door on the right. Klaus pokes his head into the first room. It is an office. There is a large desk in the centre and cabinets lining the wall behind it. It doesn't look very useful. As the group moves to the second room, Klaus pauses in the doorway. He looks back and nods to Isaac. Both men enter this room in the same manner as they did the foyer, stepping to the side and surveying the new room. Klaus waves the others in and walks in further to look at the shelves. Each shelf has rows of long, cylindrical jars with metal screw caps. They appear to be labelled. Shoku walks the length of the shelving unit, staring up at the cylinders in awe. Maeve is standing back with her hand over her heart, looking painfully hurt. Pax quietly starts reading the names on each cylinder. Maya and Gabe walk in and intuitively walk to the second shelf.

"Every canister has a name on it," Pax says. "Why would each one have a name?" As soon as Pax says it, each of the seven travellers feels a shot of understanding. Each cylinder holds someone's internal clock. They all take a step back and stare at the vastness of the room and the number of cylinders set up on the shelves. There must be thousands of cylinders. It is truly overwhelming. Gabe staggers forward, and whispers, "Michael?" He raises his hands up toward the shelving, looking horrified. He starts to scan the names within the immensity of the long shelving units.

Each of the seven travellers step forward and start to scan the names.

"Wait," Maeve yells, "don't touch them! I have a strange feeling that once you touch it, we will need to seek them out. Let's focus on Michael first and then we can come back here later with help to start finding the others."

The others nod and walk the length of the shelves, searching for Michael's name.

"Michael Guillaume, Michael Guillaume!" Pax yells. "I found it!" Pax stands in front of Michael's cylinder in the second section of shelving. He is pointing and grinning. The group crowds in and looks at it in amazement.

"Okay, everyone," Gabe takes a deep breath, "circle up. We have no idea what is about to happen."

The group circles up, ready for Gabe to turn around and join the circle, keeping Maya in the middle. Everyone has a glimmer of hope that holding Michael's internal clock might provide some insight as to where he might be.

Gabe speaks, "Let's set the intention that this canister can help us find Michael. Also set the intention that we are bound in this circle. We are protected and camouflaged for the duration of our journey. Set the intention that we travel together." Gabe's right hand hovers over the cylinder, shaking.

Maeve guides the group to send loving, supportive energy to Gabe as he makes this hard transition. The group tunes in and holds space for Gabe, linking metaphorical hands and radiating positive white light into their circle. Gabe closes his fingers around the canister and lifts the cylinder from its perch, sliding it off of the shelf and into his left hand. He turns slowly, cupping the cylinder like it is the most precious thing he has ever held.

The circle feels the pain immediately. The torturous, screeching screams of agony. Gabe recoils and shakes at hearing his brother's anguish. The group resists placing their hands over their ears. Their eyes squint in discomfort. They fortify their luminescence, focusing all of their energy to Gabe and Michael.

Michael's internal clock begins to glow, absorbing the healing energy as it infuses it into its cells. The cells begin to vibrate and the canister starts to shake in Gabe's hands. Within seconds the circle begins to spin again, and is pulled down another tunnel. As they start to shift, Maya hears a faint voice calling out, "Don't forget to find those of us who are lost!" It repeats and begins to get louder, as more and more voices join in, "Don't forget to find those of us who are lost! Don't forget to find those of us who are lost!" The circle looks to Maya as they are pulled down the tunnel. Unsure what to say, Maya looks to Maeve for guidance. Maeve nods in agreement and quietly communicates, "We will be back, kind souls. We will be back. Love and infinite peace; we will return."

FINDING

THE CIRCLE ARRIVES in a destitute land, sur-rounded by blackened dirt and burnt-out trees. Gabe looks around frantically, wondering why the group was sent to these ruins. That's when he saw Michael, lying on the ground, near dead, blackened by dirt and surrounded by rodent carcasses.

"Michael!" Gabe yells, breaking the circle and running toward Michael. The circle follows to hold space. Gabe lifts Michael into his arms, screaming at the heavens, "Michael!"

Maeve calls the circle to come together to heal. The circle immediately tunes in to Maeve's guidance.

"Inhale, greater connection, exhale to surround Michael's physical and emotional body," Maeve guides them. "Inhale, loving white healing energy. Exhale all of this loving, white energy into Michael. Now focus on his heart chakra. Focus on filling his heart with green and pink light energy. Breathe into Source Energy, expanding his heart chakra with each breath."

The group continues with this pattern until Maeve gives the next direction. "Now focus on growing that energy out from Michael's heart chakra down into the solar plexus, sending him great strength and power to overcome this adversity."

After holding this breath for a few minutes, Maeve guides the group to continue down to the sacral chakra by sending love and light to all relationships that Michael holds dear to his heart. Maeve also calls the group to focus on collectively discovering creative solutions to this situation. After a few minutes radiating here, Maeve guides the group to go further still, into Michael's root chakra and grounding down into Mother Earth. The channel of light grows stronger with each breath. Once the circle has effectively grounded him, Maeve guides the group up to his throat chakra, where she calls on the members to clearly reiterate their intention for Michael to heal his ejected cells and integrate them back within his body. After holding space, Maeve guides the group up to his third eye chakra, where Maeve changes her tone and speaks directly to Michael, urging him to reconnect to his intuitive higher self. Finally, Maeve guides the group up to Michael's crown chakra, where she again points out the channel of light now reaching up to the heavens to connect with Michael's Source Energy.

While the group continues to focus on sending healing energy to Michael, Gabe holds him in his arms, his internal clock vibrating nearby on the ground.

"Gabe," Maeve says, "Michael is ready. You will need to open the canister and hold it near Michael."

Gabe looks up, a little shocked beneath his tears, and nods. He releases Michael from his hold and places him back on the dark earth. He reaches for the cylinder and lifts it over Michael's body. As he untwists the canister, the cylinder begins to vibrate more. The golden cells of Michael's internal clock are moving faster now, ricocheting off each other and the sides of the canister at a rapid pace. As Gabe lifts the lid off the canister, the cells bounce and jostle to the top of the cylinder and out into the air.

The cells intuitively know where to go, to the body they had been separated from, just inches away. The yellow and orange bubbles arc out of the cylinder and down toward Michael's chest, assimilating back into their keeper. Michael's chest rises off the ground even though he looks as if he is still sleeping or dead. His shoulders and arms roll back toward the earth, supporting this arch. His body shakes as it fills with this lost matter. The circle watches in amazement, having been unsure if they could save Michael.

As the last of the cells are absorbed into Michael's body, he relaxes back down to the earth. His breathing is deep. The circle waits, holding space for Michael, hoping this amalgamation of his body and internal clock will allow him to recover. Gabe hovers over Michael, placing his hands directly on Michael's heart chakra.

"I'm here, brother. I'm here. I've got you," Gabe says.

Michael's eyelids start to flutter. He winces in pain and rolls onto his side, buckling at the waist and landing in a fetal position. "Gabe," Michael whispers. "You found me!"

"I got you, buddy." Gabe lies down beside Michael, cocooning him in a long embrace. The boys are both crying in relief.

After a few minutes, Gabe sits up and coaxes Michael to join him. Gabe wraps Michael in his arms, propping him up. Michael looks around in disgust at his home for the past few months. He turns to Maya.

"Thank you. I can't even imagine what would have happened to me if you hadn't agreed to come on this mission."

Maya grins, and runs toward Michael. She kneels on the ground and hugs him, burying her face in his shoulder. She is crying big ugly tears of joy, tears of sadness, and tears of relief.

"Michael! It's so nice to finally meet you!" They both giggle and hug again.

Michael turns to the rest of the circle. "Thank you all so much for coming. I cannot begin to thank you enough." He looks to Gabe. "What has happened with the Pruner and the Collective?"

"The Collective came together almost immediately and collaborated across all time-space realities. It was brilliant to see. To say the energy was amazing is an understatement. We sought out the Pruner, but he actually came looking for us. We were able to surround him in light upon entry into our awareness. Then we began filling him with positive energy. In the end, it overpowered him and he was reintegrated into Source Energy. It was really quite spectacular. The Collective continues to search out all of the Clippers to heal them, raise their vibration, and teach them the proper ways of working with Source Energy," Gabe explains. "Many are grateful for this training, some are resistant … and there is another problem." Gabe pauses.

Michael looks up. "What's that?"

"The place where we found your internal clock … there are thousands of others." Gabe lets the magnitude of the situation sink in. "We will need to recruit more of the Collective to go and save them."

"Well," Michael says quickly, "What are we waiting for? Let's go!"

"Right," agrees Gabe. "Let's head back to our meeting place and get you cleaned up while we recruit."

"Great idea! I really stink … I need a toothbrush and some clean clothes … and I need some real food!" Michael laughs. Then, with a look of fear on his face, he asks, "Gabe, are you sure I'm going to be able to shift?"

"I would think so," Gabe says, "but we are going to link up our energies and keep you and Maya inside our circle of protection, so it's a nonissue at this stage. We can look more into it later, okay?" Gabe smiles and ruffles Michael's hair.

Michael walks over to the circle and joins Maya in the middle, reaching for her hand. Gabe closes the circle and looks to each of the protectors.

"Shall we?" he prompts.

THE RETURN

THE CIRCLE SETS the intention to be protected and guarded while they travel, carrying Michael back to their meeting place of April fifteenth, 2017, ten a.m. in Takayama Market.

With the power of group consciousness, the circle arrives back in the market within seconds, circumventing the long tunnel ride.

"Shoko," instructs Gabe, "can you please go with Michael to grab some toiletries and get him set up for a shower? We will connect to the Collective to call for more volunteers."

"*Hai,*" Shoku bows, then nods to Michael and says, "Let's go this way. My uncle has a shop on the next street with an apartment upstairs. He is connected to the Collective and won't wonder why we are in 2017." Michael leans on Shoku as they walk down the street, chatting about the different trinkets that are being sold in the market in order to lighten the mood.

The circle reforms around Maya, and the group sinks into meditation. Once they are connected to the Collective, Gabe checks in with Haylen.

She explains, "Many of the Clippers had been hypnotized to follow the Pruner, and once they were released from his hold, they were grateful to start learning healing techniques and the rightful way of using Source Energy. Each Clipper who volunteered to participate in training has been matched up with a mentor. We will check in with each partnership frequently over the next month, and then monthly over the next year. The Clippers who were more ingrained in their support to the Pruner are resisting mentorship. We are holding those we have located in space as we continue to heal them from a distance and try to release their mind control. In the case of the Clippers who are more elusive, we will continue to put out feelers to find them."

"Were you able to find the machine?" asks Gabe.

"No, not yet. How was your mission to find Michael?" Haylen asks.

"We were successful!" Gabe happily reports. "But he was near death. Plus, there are many more beings to find who have been separated from their internal clocks. We need more volunteers to help us. Ideally, we need thirty or forty volunteers to start. We need at least five or six protectors and four healers, plus anyone else willing to help."

"That shouldn't be too hard," Haylen says. "Let's take the next few minutes to broadcast that request to the Collective. I would recommend that we not take any of the new mentors, as their efforts are needed elsewhere."

"Perfect," Gabe says, and turns his attention to the Collective to broadcast his request.

RECRUITS

WHEN THE BROADCAST is finished, Gabe has thirty-three more volunteers. He gives them the location of the meeting place and they all tune in and shift.

When they arrive at the meeting place, Gabe starts forming groups. He chooses one of the original team members, plus five or six of the new volunteers, ensuring each group has at least one healer and one protector. By this point, Shoku and Michael have returned and Gabe sets Shoku up with the new recruits. He keeps Michael and Maya working next to him, organizing the groups.

He looks around at the forty light beings and says, "Everyone, I think we need to shift to a better practice space and meeting ground. Please shift to Ancaster Little League Park, June thirteenth, 2019, one-fifteen p.m. School will still be in, so there won't be anyone there during the day and we can use it as a quick training ground and future meeting place."

The whole group nods as if in unison. They turn inward to ground and shift immediately, meeting in the ballpark. The volunteers spread out in the field and shuffle into their small groups, each with their group leader. There are four groups of seven, travelling under Shoko, Pax, Maeve, and Klaus. Isaac's group only has six, but he is both a strong healer and protector so they should be okay. Gabe, Maya, and Michael will remain at the ballpark to continue recruiting and to set up showers and meals for everyone.

Gabe looks out at the field and asks everyone to rein it in for a discussion. He sets the intention that his voice is magnified loud enough for all to hear. "When we begin," he bellows over the field, "set the intention that your circle remains intact throughout all shifting with protection and camouflage until you return here. The guides of each group will walk you through the whole process, from setting protection to finding the Pruner's headquarters and choosing a cylinder which will contain someone's internal clock.

"We believe that there may be great power in rescuing someone you know. We highly recommend finding a name that one of your four or five supporters recognize for the first few trips. Allow the person who knows the afflicted to take the canister off the shelf and hold it for the duration of the rescue. It will be their job to untwist the top and hold the canister overtop of the victim once the healer has guided you through raising the victim's vibration. We believe there may be comfort and solace in awakening to a familiar face.

"Oh, I'm so sorry, I got ahead of myself." Gabe says. "Let me backtrack. When you are standing in front of the shelves and find the cylinder your group has chosen, you will create a circle near the canister. The person who will be taking the canister off the shelf will stand in front of it and you will all form the circle out from them. As they take the canister from the shelf, they will step into the centre of the circle. The group will set the intention to find and heal this person.

"The internal clock will begin to vibrate in an attempt to find its owner. The cylinder should guide you to find its resting place. When you arrive, set up a healing circle around the person. The protector will set a safety around the circle and the healer will lead an energetic charge. Once the person is radiating from all chakra points, the healer will notify whomever is holding the cylinder to open the canister. Do this overtop of the person. Then you will hold space for the person to heal.

"This is where we are hoping you have the same experience that we had with Michael. The cells contained in the cylinder should vibrate out and join with their owner. The victim should begin to repair and further heal at this point. Once they have healed enough to sit up, embrace them and give them time to assimilate to their healing. When they are ready to travel, place the person in the middle with their friend, and bring them back here to be examined first and complete further healing before returning home.

"We do not know much about this situation. We had success with Michael, but we do not know if everyone can be rescued. We do not know if it is too late. We do not know what will happen when returning the internal clocks. We do not know if these people will ever be able to travel on their own again. But we do know we have to try. We know that with love and light we have the ability to heal and potentially rescue many people. We know that all of our energy is connected. We know we have to try!

"If you come across a being for whom you cannot raise their vibration, do not try to connect their internal clock. Try to protect them in your circle and bring them home. I will try to recruit many healers on my next visit to the Collective. We can have them try to save or transmute any resistant souls. We can't begin to imagine the hardships that these souls have endured over the past few months. Please be patient with them." Gabe looks at Michael and nearly breaks into tears. "Isaac and his team will be seeking out the pincer machine that removes internal clocks. If anyone hears anything about this weapon, please share the location with us as soon as possible.

"One last thing," Gabe pauses and then continues. "The images that you are about to see are horrifying. The level of starvation and destitution these people have gone through is barbaric. The sheer vastness of internal clocks on the shelves feels palpable. I do not tell you this to scare you, but rather to numb some of the effects upon encountering its vastness for the first time. I urge you to hold the light as you enter into this journey. Hold the light and be the strength." Gabe pauses and looks out at the volunteers.

"Are there any questions?" Gabe leaves an opening for concerns. Everyone stares at him.

"While you are gone, Michael, Maya, and I will set up space for your return. We will find more healers, food, and shower facilities. The next time you come back, we will have a full setup here. Set your intention to come back to the first dimension at this park." Gabe pauses and looks around.

"Well, if there aren't any questions or concerns, circle up!" Gabe raises his hands in the air. "I wish you all the best—luck, speed, safety, and health. With love, light, and infinite peace. We are here for you if you need us. Hold the light." Gabe raises his hands into prayer position and lifts his hands to his forehead, sending his team a silent prayer.

"Hold the light," the volunteers respond, and turn inward to their circles, listening to their guides.

As each group begins to shift to the Pruner's headquarters, Maya sees their travel residue as they pan away. She is sure she hears it again: "Don't forget to find those of us who are lost. Don't forget to find those of us who are lost."

"We're coming," Maya confirms. "We're coming. I promise. Hold the light."

CPSIA information can be obtained
at www.ICGtesting.com
Printed in the USA
BVHW052157041122
651116BV00003B/6

9 781039 146051